CHAMPIONS OF LOVE

Goemon knelt on the mat and bowed to the woman who was sitting formally on a cushion near the window. She wore a light summer robe that opened more than was strictly necessary at the throat.

'I have been out of sorts for days, doctor,' she said, 'and I would like to avail myself of your services.'

She stretched out a smooth, round, pale arm for him to take her wrist pulse. He then leaned over to take the pulse at her neck, and her hand fell casually into his lap.

'You must see about my back, too,' she breathed, and with a single motion turned and let her robe drop. The back was a smooth expanse, her neck was long, and a single strand of hair from her elaborate coiffure decorated her nape. He placed his hands on her cool skin and the medical gesture turned to an exploring stroke, which led from the nape down to the swell of the hips. She arched her back and hissed. He ran his hands more familiarly over her and then under her arms to seize her breasts. Full nipples leaped erect at the touch of his fingers.

'Yes, doctor,' she murmured as she covered his hands with her own, 'that is where it hurts . . .'

CHAMPIONS OF LOVE

Anonymous

NEXUS

A Nexus Book
Published in 1989
by the Paperback Division of
W. H. Allen & Co Plc
26 Grand Union Center,
338 Ladbroke Grove, London W10

Reprinted 1990

Printed in Great Britain by
Cox & Wyman Ltd, Reading, Berks.

ISBN 0 352 32378 7

Champions
of
Love

CHAPTER 1

The young man clutched at his loose trousers as he watched the old man enter the maid. She lay there, struggling awhile while the thick pale flesh pole entered her. The old man pushed on inexorably, his massive member disappearing gradually in her dark cleft, barely painted by a brush of black hair. The lad could see the sweat on her brow as finally the hair at the root of the man's cock melded with her own, and she took the full weight of the old sea rover on her slim body. The old man began moving. He drew his prick out so that it showed over her thighs and then thrust himself home again with a grunt. She raised her brown stocky legs over his massive back. He thrust his tongue into her mouth as she began moaning, whether with the weight or with pleasure, the youth could not tell. The old man's rhythm increased, and the girl raised her body to meet his. The rice bales on which she was lying shifted under the pounding pressure. The man slid his hands down her haunches and hid them under her ass. She moaned again and the tempo of the fuck increased. He changed the speed of his thrusts. They became slower but deeper, almost brutal. His belly slapped down onto the

1

girl's and she cried 'Please, please' asking him to stop or to continue, the watcher could not tell. The man raised his head from the girl's and his face became red and apoplectic. 'I'm coming. I'm coming . . .' he cried. His loins slammed into the girl's and she raised her head in ecstasy. The man shot off his load and his body jerked with the power of it. The girl drew her fingers hard against the man's shoulders, but made no impression with her short nails on the thick hide, darkened by sun and wind.

The old man lay on the girl as if dead. His thick white-streaked beard tickled her shoulder. At last, impatiently, she twitched her leg. He grunted and rolled off her. He was a giant of a man, and her figure, a golden brown colour, looked like a doll's compared to his. He tweaked a dark brown nipple on the almost flat breast, and she stretched voluptuously, then lay her hand on the limp soggy prick beside her. He grinned, said something in a low voice the watcher could not hear, and stood up. After adjusting his clothing, he walked out of the barn. The girl lay there, her flat-nosed face calm, her eyes almost closed.

The young man stared at the wet dribble on the cracked wooden wall of the barn before him. He shivered, and then his eyes hardened in resolve. Restoring his still hard prick to his trousers, he walked around to the entrance to the barn. He could still see the tall broad figure of his father walking away towards the villa they lived in. He marched into the barn to confront the maid. She had dressed by then, wrapping her gown tightly around her, and was now adjusting her sash. She

2

looked at him as if in surprise, then, noting the look on his face, grinned slyly.

'Well, young master, enjoyed the show?'

The young man tried to swallow, found his throat dry. Faced with the reality, he could barely get a word out of his mouth. His hands leaped forward as if on their own, and he seized the girl's small breasts for an instant, their prominent nipples burning his palms. She slipped aside, slapped his groping hands.

'No, no. Still too small for me. I prefer bigger men.' Her hand snaked out and grabbed him by the crotch. Not hard enough to really hurt, the movement was a surprise to the youth, who was still confused between his lust and his inexperience. She ran to the door.

'When you grow older, young master . . .' she flipped her skirts at him, 'and bigger!' and with a giggle, she was gone. The boy was left alone in the barn with his painful erection.

Okiku was breathing evenly, unlike the man she was riding. Her thighs gripped him unmercifully as her hands traced patterns on the muscled chest. The man beneath her she had met on the road, and liking his looks, had made advances – breathed harshly and arched his back. He tried to stab her innards with his prick, but she rode so skilfully he was never able to reach the orgasm he craved. His prick, she noted, did not give her as much pleasure as she had hoped. She rammed herself hard down on him, leaning forward to bring her clit into contact with his erect maleness. That last motion was too much for him. He exploded wildly, wetting her insides with a torrent of juice. With disappointment she felt his prick shrink inside her as soon as he had finished. She ejected his cock with her interior muscles and rose to her feet. He rose after her, fumbling at his loincloth.

'Well sweetie,' he said. 'How was it? Good huh?'

She snorted in derision. 'It was probably the worst fuck I've ever had.' She turned to get her clothes and brushed the leaves off her knees.

'Oh yeah?' he said. He had the rough accents of a southerner. 'Come here, and I'll show you what's what.'

'Oh go and play with yourself.' Okiku was too confident of her own abilities to assume the attitude of servility and helplessness the world expected of women. Angered, he tried to seize her and instead of pulling back, she leaned forward. With her two hands she grasped his thumb and little finger, and then throwing her weight to one side, she held her elbows and shoulders rigid. There was a snap and the man screamed in a high-pitched voice. His wrist dangled. Quickly, Okiku snaked a hand into the cloth belt he wore around his middle. While riding him she had felt the wallet there. before the hurt man could do a thing, she had leapt back, heavy wallet in her hand. She extracted the three silver pieces it contained and threw it contemptuously back in his face. Grabbing her clothes, walking stick and bundle, she skipped back through the bushes in the direction of the dimly seen village of Miura, tugging her robe around her as she walked. Not satisfied except financially by her exercise, she rubbed her mound pensively as she walked, the thrills continuing to race up her spine the closer she slid down the slopes to the village.

Rosamund woke gradually. The pounding she noticed first was that of the surf, roaring in behind her as it had roared when the ship went down. She had thrown off her habit when she tried to swim to shore, and was now naked but for her shift. The warm sand gritted on her fair skin. She picked herself up, spitting out sand grains. She was in a small rounded cove, bounded on either end by piles of grey rock. Before her rose a steep slope covered with bushes and trees. Feathery plumes of some paler green growth she could not identify waved in the wind. She rose completely and took stock of herself. Her crucifix and habit were gone. Besides a thin transparent shift, she had only herself. Full white breasts topped by cherry-like nipples hid a smoothly sloping stomach which funnelled into a generous stretch of hair, a darker version of the gold of her head. Long legs, pale except for their backs where they burned from overexposure, completed the ensemble she could see.

She wondered where she was. Her upbringing and subsequent life had been sheltered. She knew little of the world beyond that which she had been taught at the convent. She had been on her way to Cathay, to establish a mission to the heathen Chinese, when the ship had foundered in a storm. Perhaps she was already in China, or, much better, the Philippine Islands, ruled by His Most Catholic Majesty Philip III of Spain. That would be nice, she decided, being rescued by a handsome don, who would take her away from her expected fate as a nun.

Still unsteady, she began walking towards the shade of the trees before her. As she approached, she stepped on a dry branch which broke under her feet. A human figure popped up suddenly from behind a bush. She gave a short surprised yelp, and then paused to look before fleeing. The young man had a smooth bronze-coloured face with almond-shaped eyes and high cheekbones. He wore a blue kerchief folded over his head in a peculiar three-cornered fashion, loose colourful clothes, and carried a short curved sword in his sash. A staff with a gnarled top, and a bag of chequered blue cloth, lay at his feet.

Goemon, for so he called himself now, watched the apparition before him. She was, he decided, a woman of the Southern Barbarians. But she was dressed, or undressed. . . . He licked his lips slowly. The pale cotton shift barely went to her knees, and being slightly wet, was transparent throughout.

He reached out a hand and said, 'Don't be afraid.' Mistaking his motion and not understanding his words, Rosamund turned and ran. Goemon, intending to explain, leaped after her. She ran across the sands, her shift flying. He closed in on her easily, but as he closed, he began noticing the details of her body. Her high pale ass swung before him, now hidden, now exposed. Beneath it he could see the tufts of the delicate golden beard she wore between her legs. Her heavy breasts enticed him as they bobbled from side to side. He made a flying leap and they tumbled together into

6

the sand, he on top. At the feel of her skin, his
prick rose up and knocked against her exposed
belly. Not pausing, he loosened the ties of his trousers and the magnificent erection swung free. She
tried to push him away and her hand slipped,
sliding down to grab his swaying stick unintention-
ally. They both gasped. He with pleasant anticipation, she with surprise. The prick was almost the
thickness of her wrist. She stared at it in dread
mixed with anticipation. Having seen the anticipation gleam in his eyes, she knew what lay in
store for her. The prick rose, a dark brown column
nesting in black hairs. Below it dangled a soft
looking, pulsing bag covered with the same coarse
hairs. The wide, dark tip seemed to stare at her
blindly from one eye. She shrieked and let go, but
he held her hand fast and brought her soft white
palm up and along the length of the shaft. He
was grinning now. She struggled and squirmed to
extricate herself, but his knees forced her legs apart.
He wedged himself between her knees as she struggled desperately to escape. He pushed. His prick
missed its target and ploughed its sticky way up
her pussy. Excited by the roughness of the hairs he
tried again. Her movements while trying to escape
excited him. He pinned her to the ground with his
body, and stuck his fingers into the pink opening
of her cunt. Dry and virginal, the cunt twitched in
his grasp as she screamed. He laid his index finger
on the nub of her clitoris, and folded the thick
lips over his finger with delight. The little hole
moistened lightly. He kept on moving his hand
while pinning her down with his body. Releasing
her hands, which commenced to beat on his shoul-

7

ders ineffectually, he pushed her thighs apart. Spread beneath him, thighs wide, the pink lips framed with gold wisps presented a target that could not be missed. He slammed his body forward from his position on all fours. His prick hit the mark and his lance entered the smooth channels of her body. He surged upwards and inwards, digging toes into sand as his prick burrowed into her belly. Their hair meshed and he drove their pelvic bones together. He rotated his loins in delight, as she lay beneath him moaning.

His prick began the familiar pumping motion, almost too excited to control. He drew his prick out almost to the tip, and thrust home again. Again and again he repeated his action, as her pained stare began to change into a look of not-unpleasant surprise. Before she could explore this sensation further or begin to understand it, he exploded. Clouds of sperm flew from his prick, inundating her insides, smoothing their membranes. He bored into her, his eyes open and staring in a fit, his hands seizing and crushing her tits.

When it was over, he lay on her belly, idly sucking her nipples. She whimpered and moved slightly beneath him. Obligingly he rolled off her and smiled happily. He examined the blood-and-come-stained thighs, the wet matted hairs, and smiled with satisfaction and delight. His hand roved over her full breasts, smacking her fingers aside as she tried to stop him. He then delved again into her sopping cunt, spreading the hairs. She tried to move away from his touch. A cuff on the nearest fat firm breast put an end to that.

'You are interesting-looking,' he said, and leaned

over to suck a nipple that rose cheekily near his face. 'In a while I'll do it again, and this time you will enjoy it.'

She answered in a language he did not know. He tried Dutch.

She looked at him in surprise. The nuns who had raised her had spoken High German, and the language he was speaking sounded like a variant of that. After a fashion, his hands still exploring her ripe body, they began to communicate.

'That was terrible, a sin . . .'

'So, you are a kirisitan?'

The question surprised her for a minute but then, 'Yes, a Christian. A Christian nun,' or at least, she thought, a novice. 'It is sinful to abuse me as you have done.'

He grinned at her. 'Here in Nippon, the kirisitan sect is banned. I would not admit to membership in it if I were you. You would be crucified.'

She shuddered with fear. The thought of holy martyrdom rose before her eyes for a moment, and was then overcome by the fear of death.

'What is this horrible place where men . . . where men . . .' She couldn't express the word in her limited German, and even in her native tongue, the word would not have come easily to her lips.

He grinned again and patted her belly. 'Before you go to the cross, I will make use of you again.' She stared in fascinated horror as the limp glistening length of his prick began swelling again.

Again he spread her thighs, taking in with his eyes the sight of her sopping cunt. Then, leaning forward, he lapped at the lips and commenced sucking at the prominently erect clitoris. Her hands groped in the sand, not knowing how to react to the sensations – painful but overcast with a new emotion she knew somehow was sinful – the lingual massage roused in her. He delighted in his power. Drunk with the smell and taste of her awakening cunt, he fell prostrate by the blow from the piece of driftwood she had found in the sand.

The chase this time was a repetition of the first, but both participants moved slower. The blood from his scalp wound was absorbed by his kerchief, but the pain was absorbed by the pleasure of pursuit as the white thighs, now speckled with a few drops of blood, fled before him. He caught up with her in the shade of the woods. He threw her on the ground and buried his face in her heaving and sweaty breasts. Her gasps were compounded of pain, fear, and a new-found delight as he bit her nipples and tits. The nipples sprang erect. She closed her thighs forcefully, but they were dragged apart. He shoved his rampant prick into her hole. The burning sensation from the unhealed wound overcame her for a minute, but then the delight of the sharply biting teeth and sucking lips, and above all, the monster serpent in her pussy, drove all thoughts from her head. Her head began twisting from side to side, a twin to her hips that swivelled and tried to swallow more of the meat shoved into her. Unfamiliar waves rose from her cunt to her spine and head. The pleasure became unbearable as he bored into her. She dug her heels into the ground, not to push him off now, but to force more of him into her. The pulse of the drilling rod did not disappear, but added to her pleasure as she screamed.

10

Goemon collapsed on her. He closed his eyes, allowing his prick and come to trickle gradually out of her cunt and down the crack of her ass. The power of his orgasm made his head throb at the wound, and he slid off her perfect white belly unconscious.

She shook him off and wiped herself the best she could with her shift. Searching the beach, she found his loose coat-like shirt, and after donning it, she began climbing the steep slopes, getting away from the events that had overtaken her.

CHAPTER 2

Looking at his parents as they ate the evening meal, Jiro could hardly believe what had passed in the barn an hour before, while his mother had gone to the temple. His father, a giant of a man, ate with his usual gusto and barbarian manners. After twenty years in the country, his father still acted the barbarian sometimes. His mother, a small, smooth-skinned woman wearing a silk kimono as befitted the wife of a nobleman, seemed a porcelain doll beside him. Jiro's thoughts drifted inevitably to the sight in the barn as he heard the maid move about in the kitchen behind him.

His father grunted and belched slightly.

'Well, Jerry, how are your ship drawings coming?'

Jiro hated being called Jerry, but his father ruled all their lives with his own brand of humour and force. Though his second son had inherited some of his size and colour, he had inherited none of Anjin of Miura's skill at shipbuilding or enginering. The man once known as Will Adams scowled as his half-Japanese, half-English son bowed and muttered that his assigned work would soon be finished. His elder son away at Edo, he wished that

13

the younger lunk he had privately named Gerald, so much like him in size and temperament, would also be a success.

After dinner, the young man stretched, settled his swords into place in his sash, and begged leave to go out. His mother cast him a sharp look. Mirus villagers did not practice nightwalking – visiting girls for sex in the middle of the night – and she could not help wonder what her son was up to.

In truth, all Jiro wanted to do was relieve himself. His prick was heavy, and he knew there was no chance of catching the maid outside at this time. He wandered off into the bamboo grove behind the house, climbing the slope towards the red-painted shrine of hachiman at the hill's summit. As he walked, seeking concealment, he practised the 'silent tread' taught all the samurai boys by the fencing master. He slipped through the grove silently, and dipped into a small, bush-surrounded hollow. His prick stood out in splendour as he examined it. He rubbed it experimentally, and the reddish staff quivered. As he rubbed again, he thought he heard a movement. Before he could cover himself, he saw the glint of something move in the moonlight. Looking closer, and sliding his feet silently, he saw a bent-over form dressed in a dirty brown shirt. The shirt was hiked up, displaying a round white bottom cleft by darkness. For a moment, Jiro was back in the barn. Without volition he slid forward. The ass before him moved, as its owner, intent on something before her, peered through parted bushes at the small shrine building.

Almost without thought now, Jiro's hands moved. He dropped his trousers, loincloth, and loose shirt. He knelt behind the figure. With deliberation and speed, he seized the figure by neck and hip. Before she could do more than gasp, his prick was probing at her backside. Two incredibly soft and large mounds guided his pole between them. He jerked his loins forward hard and his rigid cock found an opening which yielded only slowly to efforts. He felt through the fingers of his left hand that the woman was about to scream, and he tightened his fingers warningly. Suddenly the ring of muscle gave, as the crest of Jiro's prick completed its penetration and he slid up into paradise. He moaned in delight while she struggled ineffectually beneath him. The weight of his body forced her hand away from the lips of her cunt as she needed to support the sudden weight. Jiro's feeling himself well lodged in her and marvellously supported, began to take stock of his surroundings. His hands snaked around a plump soft belly and explored a full thicket of soft curly hairs. His fingers moved downwards through the mossy growth until he found the beautiful, slick, mysterious folds that were hidden among the hairs. Barely knowing what to do or how to handle it, he let his finger pads explore the sticky folds. He explored some more, and each movement of his hands through the unknown bumps and ridges of flesh brought a trembling response from the girl, squatting on all fours beneath him. He explored further, finding his own large ball-bag swinging beneath, and the root of his manhood disappearing in a ring of muscle. To withdraw now might precipitate another struggle, and in any case, was unthinkable under the circumstances. He ploughed on.

His prick moved up and down in the unfamiliar channel as he got into a rhythm. He explored the folds of her cunt with his right hand, gently probing with the pads of his fingers, sending one digit up the moist channel between the soft plump lips, occasionally exploring the feel of his own prick as it moved in and out of her. Inadvertently, his probing fingers found the protuberance of her clitoris. At the first touch, her body quivered. Jiro, sunk in his own pleasure, his eyes closed, barely noticed. She moved her body unconsciously to encourage contact, and his fingers pinched the joy button again. This time he noticed as she let out a breathless moan. It was not long before his inexpert fumbles became sure strokes as he gently, then more roughly, stroked the inside of her lips and the slightly hardening clit.

The girl under him began to writhe slowly to his rhythm. The two fat mounds of her ass burned his belly, and in less time than he thought possible, the pressure on his balls became unbearable. His hips jerked uncontrollably. His whole body seemed concentrated in one spot. He rammed her again and again in a frenzy, not forgetting to tease her clitoris as he moved. His spasms began somewhere down along his spine. This was nothing like the pale orgasms when he jerked himself off. This was the real thing, he thought as he exploded within her, inundating her interior with his thick cream. Unwilling to let go, he was suddenly conscious that the girl, far from fighting him for the last few moments, was actually gasping in pleasure. His young prick still erect, he continued probing her. His right hand continued milking her clitoris, while

16

his left moved away from her throat and grasped an available hanging breast. The breast was the largest Jiro could imagine. He had seen, even managed to feel, female breasts before in the public bath. But the breast he held was larger than the palm of his hand, full, and with a large round erect nipple that he pinched in delight.

Conscious of the woman's body beneath him as she approached her own climax, he also became conscious of his surroundings. Suddenly the picture before his face became clear, as well as the reason for the raped girl's silence.

Through the thin screen provided by a bush, he could see the small clearing before the red-painted shrine of Hachiman. In the clearing danced a nude female demon. His eyes traced the slim curves of her ripe female body, the shadow cleft between her legs with a small heart-shaped patch of hair, smooth-muscled belly and conical tits. On a long slim neck rested a hideous head: white as chalk, grinning red, long horns projecting from the forehead. Startled for a moment, Jiro recognised a dance mask, as the figure continued its unusual steps.

The dancer, unconscious of the two observers, held a straight sword in one hand which she waved slowly to a beat only she could hear. With her other hand she caressed her body slowly, lingering over her nipples in turn, stroking her buttocks, descending slowly to tickle the spot between her legs. Never losing the rhythm, she was slowly approaching the climax she had not achieved earlier because of a useless male.

Jiro's juices rose once again at the sight of the

17

dancer. He began moving faster and faster into his companion. His hands now probed deep into her cunt, now squeezed her magnificent breasts. He squeezed the two hills together, then pulled them apart, bringing a small moan of distress from the figure beneath him. Soon he approached his climax. He stuck his hand into her cunt, twisting her prominent clit between rigid fingers. She twitched as she felt pain and pleasure mingle familiarly.

This time, as he came, he felt the girl beneath him jerk and force her buns backs against him, grinding her ass into his belly, forcing the breath from his lungs as he shot his load into her for a second time. Shudder after shudder seized her as she came too. She gave a jerk as the final spasm caught her, and uncontrollably moaned out loud in her pleasure before subsiding beneath him.

The dancing figure in the clearing, hearing the moan, left off in mid-step. In three quick strides she had leapt through the screening bush and stood over the almost comatose couple. The tip of her sword brushed Jiro's neck and the mask, glistening white as death in the moonlight, regarded them dispassionately.

CHAPTER 3

Okiku stared at the figures squatting at her feet. For a moment she was furious. Furious at being spied upon, furious at not having noticed the spies, and above all, furious at having been disturbed just before climaxing with her hand.The vision the two presented, however, soon appealed to her sense of humour. The samurai's topknot was askew, he had dropped his swords as well as his clothes in his hurry. He was a fine, large figure of youth, heavily muscled, his skin an interesting pale colour, hint of a beard on his jaws. Her left hand stole to her mound as she thought of the use she could put him to. There was a sucking, popping sound. His prick was ejected from the girl beneath him and he rolled slowly on his side. Okiku gave one look at that fine, glistening instrument and reluctantly came to the conclusion that for the moment, at least, it would do her no good whatever.

Her gaze was shifted to the girl. Rather fat, Okiku decided at first, and her skin glistened unusually in the moonlight. She nudged the girl with her foot, rolling her over. Jiro and Okiku both let out a breath. The 'fat' girl was unusually coloured and shaped, and now that they could see

19

her features, both realised she was not Japanese. Her mouth and eyes, recovering from passion, were both wide with fear. Okiku minutely examined the full body before her and her lust grew. This would be a new experience, and new experiences were something she had craved since her childhood. She kept the sword digging lightly into the young man's neck as she lowered herself next to Rosamund. She explored Rosamund's curves with her free hand, and dipped her hand curiously into the latter's cunt. This last brought a shudder from the blonde girl and a cry, 'No, please, no.'

Jiro jumped, and the sword dipped into his neck, bringing a small flow of blood.

'You speak English!!' he called in surprise.

Rosamund turned to him in shock. 'You understand me?! But . . . but who are you?'

He tried to bow but the point of the sword stopped him.

'Miura Jiro at your service,' he said in stilted, hardly used English. 'But my father calls me Jerry Adams when he's drunk. He is from England. Or was, many years ago.'

Rosamund began to cry. 'At last,' she sniffled, 'someone who can help me in this God-forsaken country. Is this truly the Japans?'

Jiro began to answer but was interrupted by Okiku.

'Shut up,' she said. 'Can you understand this woman's tongue? Then tell her that she is going to reciprocate the favour I did her.'

'What?' he asked, confusedly.

'You two spied on me and enjoyed the spectacle and one another. I have a cunt too. This plump foreign devil is going to help me come,' she grinned maliciously, 'since you obviously can't. Explain this to her.'

Jiro started to object, but the sword dug into his neck once again.

'This woman . . . wants to . . . have your body, just as I had a while ago.' He had the grace to blush.

Rosamund stared at him, confused. 'But she's a woman!'

Jiro nodded, and before he could add a word, Okiku's mouth covered Rosamund's and her long and well-trained tongue began exploring the blonde's red-lipped virginal mouth. Rosamund started to object, started to push the slimmer woman away, but was lost in the new sensation. Their tongues explored one another, licked teeth, pushed and heaved one against the other. Okiku eventually stopped to draw breath.

'Tell her I will teach her tongue sumo later, she has such a delicious mouth, but for now, she must satisfy me another way.'

Jiro compiled, but before he could explain what sumo was, Okiku had forced the other girl flat on her back. Then she rose and straddled the blonde's face. 'Lick!' she commanded, and Jiro translated the order.

Reluctantly and fearfully Rosamund obeyed the order. Her tongue licked out and barely touched the dark labial pleats. Okiku urged her on by pinching Rosamund's prominent breast and grinding her crotch into Rosamund's face. The slightly acidic taste first revolted Rosamund, but gradually, as she became used to the taste, and more importantly the smell, she began licking in earnest. Though ignorant, her strong tongue and vigorous licking strokes soon had the other woman quivering in delight. Okiku moved her body, indicating which point she wanted attended to, and Rosamund, fearful, almost choking in the close, musky dark, but with a fearful pleasure rising in her, complied.

Jiro's eyes were almost popping out of his head. His swords, toward which he was planning a break, were forgotten. His youthful prick began showing signs of energy again as it raised its head along his thigh. Noticing it, Okiku considered abandoning the delightful tongue beneath her. It would be too dangerous, she decided, and besides, the young man might give up before the right time. Instead, she motioned him forward. She leaned, and with her free hand, separated Rosamund's legs, then motioned the young man between them. He needed no further encouragement. He moved the heavy, long thighs apart and squatting between them, presented his rampant prick at the mark. Okiku's eyes widened in surprise at the sight of the magnificent instrument, and then narrowed in anticipation of the future, as wave after wave of pleasure swept through her.

This time Rosamund reacted to her thighs being parted with less reluctance. She was familiar with the prick that entered her, and raising her hips, she let Jiro's instrument work its way up her sodden canal. Less sore than the first time she was fucked, she reacted naturally, fitting the movements of her hips to those of the man, and transmitting those same motions and pleasures through her tongue and lips to the woman above her.

The three moved as one. Sword forgotten, Okiku rocked herself over Rosamund's demanding mouth, occasionally moulding a perfect breast below her, or pinching her own, sometimes scratching at the muscular shoulders of the youth before her. Jiro drove himself frantically into Rosamund's cunt. He jerked his lips, at first rhythmically, later wildly as his spasms took over his senses. He clutched at available breasts, comparing the full rounded ones and even more enticing small conical ones of the girl who had worn the demon mask. Beneath these two, Rosamund writhed in double pleasure as she gave and received simultaneously from two gloriously demanding bodies and her own.

They came together in a near explosion. All three arched their bodies simultaneously. Rosamund, almost fainting from lack of air, bit Okiku's inner thighs, forcing the slighter girl off. Jiro stretched himself full length on the leaf-covered ground, still joined to Rosamund as the dying spurts left his prick and shook his hips. Okiku rolled aside and stretched, her face near his, her thigh cradling Rosamund's blonde head. Minor spasms rocked all three of them. Unable to help himself, Jiro stretched out a gentle hand to cradle Okiku's soft cheek, while the other played alternately with Rosamund's cunt and Okiku's breasts. Rosamund, occasionally exploring Okiku's thighs with her tongue, concentrated on feeling the length of Jiro's body with her hands, finally concerning herself with the point it joined her spread legs.

'Who are you?' he asked. As the question was in Japansese, it was Okiku who answered.

'Okiku, at your service.' She giggled, and Jiro

realised she was a girl of about his own age. 'A dancer from Ugo,' she added. That province was far enough to defy immediate corroboration. She pinched the skin of his hard chest. 'You shouldn't have disturbed my dancing, and I would have treated you much better. Much better,' she breathed, as his gentle hand massaged her erect nipple. 'And you? And this beautiful foreign devil beneath me?'

'I am Miura Jiro, and my father is Miura Anjin, lord of the village of Miura and a hatamoto retainer of the Lord Shogun.' He sounded self-important even to himself and hurriedly added with a laugh 'But I am nothing at all. Only the second son . . .'

'And this?' Okiku persisted, her hand caressing the blonde head that lay on her damp brown thigh.

He shook his head in ignorance. 'I'll ask her.'

Okiku laughed. 'And you took her just like that? Without a formal introduction? Quite like a samurai.'

Not knowing what to answer, he turned his attention to Rosamund instead.

'Who are you?' he asked in English.

Rosamund told him her story. Her parents had been English Catholics, forced to leave England during King James' reign. She herself had been brought up by nuns, and upon the death of her parents, had become a novice. Her order had departed for China, to convert the heathen, and a shipwreck had precipitated her on these shores. Hesitantly she concluded, 'Is it true . . . someone told me that they execute Christians here . . .'

Jiro, translating her story to Okiku, paused for a

moment, then hesitantly, he nodded. Okiku tensed when she felt his uncertainty.

'What is it?'

'She is a kirisitan,' he said, using the Japanese term.

'A what?'

Jiro explained, and also explained that Rosamund had been a nun. 'The Lord Shogun has decreed that all kirisitan priests be put to death, by crucifixion.'

Okiku shuddered, though her thoughts were not on Rosamund, but on her own troubles. She idly caressed the soft pile of curls on her thigh, and she was rewarded with a warm soft tongue that swept up, then down the length of her wet slit. Her body shuddered, and her passion rose again. Rather than waste time worrying, she curved her body down the length of the blonde girl.

'Tell her I will do it to her this time,' she commanded Jiro.

Spellbound, he obeyed her instruction, and at her urging rolled himself from between Rosamund's pink thighs. Gently Okiku lowered her head and sniffed at the wealth of soft curls between Rosamund's legs. She rubbed her nose gently at the clitoris, and noted its size and prominence with delight. Sticking only the tip of her tongue out, she went exploring, touching the full, rosy surfaces of the outer and longer inner lips, tonguing the sweet channel briefly, lowering her tongue down to the relaxed anus. As Rosamund began to respond, Okiku opened her mouth and with a suck like a noodle-eater, she pulled in the clitoris, passing it through her lips and over her tongue. She expelled it, and repreated the motion again. Rosamund's

25

hands clawed at her back and buttocks. Leaving the clit, Okiku took the left lip of the blonde girl's cunt between her own mouth lips, and ran her mouth, licking all the time, down their length, returning to the quivering clitoris by way of the other lip. Rosamund was now trembling and moaning uncontrollably. Okiku gently bit the fleshy folds, then extruded her tongue as far as it could go into Rosamund's moist channel. She exercised her tongue in ways no prick could move, touching all the points she knew both from her own body and from previous practice, would yield the most pleasure. Rosamund threw all restraint to the winds. Her ass bounced as she shoved her cunt at Okiku's mouth, and she whimpered for more and more lingual attention as a series of orgasms started that she hoped dimly, in the still thinking part of her mind, would never end.

At this sight, Jiro noted some changes in himself. His youthful prick, uninvolved in the action that interested him intellectually to that point, gave a distinct twitch and stretched itself. His hands began wandering over the two sweating female bodies. He compared the two pairs of tits, one soft and full, the other harder and conical. He moved his hands down the crack of Okiku's ass, and his fingers paused at the tight rosebud he discovered. Not wanting to linger, he moved on, gently touching Rosamund's closed eyes, her nose, and then entering her mouth, following her tongue into the hairless cavity it was plumbing. Rosamund spared a few licks for his wandering fingers, even kissing them once, but then returned happily to the familiar muskiness of Okiku's sopping hole.

Fully aroused, Jiro rose to his knees. Commandingly, he pushed at the two bodies. Okiku obligingly rolled on top of Rosamund without losing a stroke. He knelt between her legs, then pushed gently forward. The tip of his prick came into contact with Rosamund's tongue, and his heavy, hairy bag rested on her forehead. He pushed forward, and Rosamund made a channel of her tongue, guiding the thick rigid meat into the waiting hole. On and on he pushed, for what seemed to all participants an eternity. Rosamund felt the whole length of his tremendous machine as it fed slowly into Okiku's gaping channel. Jiro felt as if his prick was entering a smooth, tight glove, just made for it. Though without much other experience, he knew a perfect fit.

When the man was all the way in, Okiku let out a long slow sigh. The cock lodged in her was what she had been waiting for all her life. Since losing her virginity, she had had many pricks up her channel. Fat and thin, long and short. This one, however was just right. She wanted it to rest there forever, as it touched and caressed all her internal membranes with a perfect touch. As if sensing the moment, both her partners remained perfectly still for a while.

At last, lust began to reassert itself. Jiro's prick gave an impatient twitch, and he began to move in the channel. Okiku responded to every move. Her internal muscles contracted rhythmically to meet the demands and comfort the remarkable piece of manhood. She shoved her ass backwards to meet him, bearing the weight of this large young man who now covered her like a huge cloak, hands grasping her breasts. Moving forward, she met with Rosamund's uneducated but willing tongue, that lapped indiscriminately at her pussy and Jiro's long rod. A push of Rosamund's hips reminded her that she had duties in that direction too, and she applied her well-trained tongue and lips to the sweet hair mound that was presented to her. In moments of conscious thought, that grew farther and farther between, she wondered at the way the foreign girl's taste differed from a native one's.

The climax that arrived was long and luxurious for the three. Okiku stretched her ass and arched her back as far as it would go. Jiro's demanding thrusts forced the two joined bodies onto Rosamund's face, and again she suffocated joyously, but this time under the pressure of two climaxing tools rather than one. For the first time in her life she tasted male cream, as the overrun from Jiro's large balls gushed out of Okiku's tight cunt. In her own turn, she wrapped voluptuous legs around Okiku's head as her spasms rocked her and gradually diminished.

CHAPTER 4

Lying huddled together on Jiro's robe, the three relaxed lovers considered their future, Jiro knew he could not let go of either the blonde or the slim dancer whose body excited him strangely. He also knew the danger Rosamund was in merely by having arrived on the shores of the island empire. He thought momentarily of asking his father, a foreigner himself originally, to help. But his father was a retainer of the Shogun, and would not conspire to break the law.

Rosamund's own feelings were complex. She had discovered a sensuality in her makeup, awakened by the man on the beach, thoroughly stimulated by this evening's encounter. She knew she should leave, even without considering the dangers of being a Christian. But the new delights she had experienced made her reluctant to depart without sampling more of what this new world and her new friends had to offer. And hidden deep in her mind was a strange thought she feared to examine. The memory of the man who had raped her on the beach, a memory she could not get out of her mind.

It remained for Okiku to make the most practical suggestion.

'We must take her to Kyushu,' she said.

'Kyushu?!' Jiro's startled response roused Rosamund and turned both girls' eyes to him. 'Why
Kyushu?' Japan's southernmost island was many
days away by boat, even futher by foot.

'There are many kirisitan there, and they might
offer her shelter. There are also some Oranda
traders there, and they will undoubtedly take her
away and save her. We must take her. I, because I
know the road, you, because as a Tokugawa
samurai, no one will question your passage – at
least as far as Osaka.'

'But . . . but my father . . . my duties . . .'

'Are you a samurai or a rabbit?' she demanded
fiercely and hit his well-muscled stomach with her
fist. 'In any case, you are the second son . . . and
their fate is well known.'

He knew what she was referring to: only the first
son inherited. He, as a younger son and an unclever
one at that, would enjoy very little of his father's
patrimony to set him on his life's road. He hurriedly
explained the situation to Rosamund. She agreed
to the proposal instantly, though he felt he could
detect a note of regret in her response.

They made their plans. Okiku would provide a
disguise for Rosamund. She was too obviously a
foreigner, and until she learned to act like a
Japanese, they would have to travel at night. Jiro
would provide some money and valuables he had
received as a gift, and would also have to take
formal leave of his father. He knew his pious
mother would support any request he might make
to go on pilgrimage to the shrine of Ise, which
would be his ostensible reason for travelling. In the

meantime, they would conceal Rosamund for the day within the shrine of Hachiman, rarely visited, and never open except during festival days.

The moonlight shone on the pillars of Hachiman's shrine as Okiku, Jiro, and even Rosamund, made the traditional handclap before the shrine to assure a successful journey. Rosamund's face was whitened, and she wore the robes of a Buddhist nun. Jiro was dressed in brown patterned robe and trousers, the latter sensibly bound by gaiters. Okiku had hidden her sword and reassumed her travelling dancer's costume.

Heading for the great Tokaido highway that led from the shogunal capital at Edo to the Imperial capital at Kyoto and the trade city of Osaka, they paralleled the rough and rocky coastline. They avoided the small fishing villages and tramped through forests of pine, small groves of bamboo, and under occasional towering cryptomeria which obscured the moonlight.

While they walked, Okiku coached Rosamund in the ways of the road. She taught her long Buddhist litanies and the proper way of holding her hands and fondling the beads. Rosamund, whose early training had been of a similar kind, took to the instruction readily, though her mind was distracted. Every time they passed a cove in the beach, her heart leaped and her legs felt watery. Though she responded eagerly during the day when Jiro entered her while Okiku licked her mound, she still felt something was missing.

They reached the small city of Kamakura on the morning of the second day. The girls concealed themselves in a bamboo thicket, while Jiro descended into the town to buy food. The girls drank from the clear mountain stream that ran nearby and fell asleep in each other's arms.

Goemon had slept uneasily for the past three nights. He had been unable to get the girl on the beach from his mind. His head still hurt abominably, but the pain roused laughter more than anger, and the laughter raised his lust. Being what and who he was, he had had many women, but none like the one on the beach. The city of Kamakura with its mouldering old temples did not serve to raise his spirits. He wandered through the streets, soliciting business without real interest. Once his eye was caught by a flash of gold. Hurrying after it he found that it was a silk covering on the head of a fat prelate. Disgusted with his own actions, he paused before a noodle stall opposite the imposing but worn facade of a large house.

'Excuse me doctor,' a high pitched voice interrupted his slurping.

He turned, the bowl still in his hands. A slim young girl stood before him, bowing. He bowed in return and returned the bowl to the stall owner.

'Excuse me doctor,' she repeated. 'My mistress has need of your services.' She waved her hand in the direction of the house on the other side of the street. Goemon, whose good nature was tickled by the sight of the young girl's earnest expression, picked up his bag and followed. He admired the slim lines of the girlish bottom that swayed before him, partly obscured by the large butterfly knot of her sash. She showed a trifle too much neck to be perfectly demure, thought Goemon.

The entry hall where he took off his straw sandals was spacious and heavily ornamented. Pebbles were set into the entrance floor, and the raised platform was a single slab of cypress of impressive dimensions. The screens, he noted as he shouted a polite 'Excuse me for disturbing you,' were of the finest paper, inlaid with watermarks. The young maid motioned him on and traipsed along a seemingly endless series of wooden corridors and stairs and grass-matted rooms. They met no one on their way.

The maid knelt by a sliding door and opened it, announcing, 'The doctor, madam.'

He entered, knelt on the mat and bowed. He had time to notice, through the wooden slats that protected the open windows, that they were in a room overlooking the street.

'Doctor, how kind of you to be bothered. Please come here and make yourself comfortable.'

The woman who had addressed him was sitting formally on a cushion near the window. There was a made-up pallet on the floor. She sat very erect in a light summer robe that opened more than was strictly necessary at the throat. About forty or thereabouts, decided Goemon, who could identify no signs of illness in her slim frame.

'What ails you, madam?' he asked in his most professional voice.

'Everywhere,' she said, pointing vaguely to her middle. 'I have been weak and out of sorts for days. My husband died two years ago, and I have been feeling unwell since. Today I saw you passing by and thought I might avail myself of your services.'

'I will have to take your pulses,' he said.

She stretched out a smooth, round, pale arm. He took her wrist pulse, and then rolled up her sleeve and took that of the upper arm. He then leaned over to take the pulse at her neck, and her hand fell casually into his lap.

'You must see about my back too,' she breathed, and with a single motion turned her back and let her robe drop. The back was a smooth expanse, showing none of the wear of age. Her neck was long and smooth, and a single strand of hair from her elaborate coiffure decorated her nape. He put his hands on her back in the necessary place, and the medical motion turned to an exploring stroke, which led from the nape down to the swell of the hips. She arched her back and hissed lightly. He ran his hands more familiarly about her back, and then under her arms to seize her breasts. Though slightly pendent, they retained enough spring to respond pleasingly to his touch. Full nipples leaped erect at the touch of his fingers.

'Yes doctor, that is where it hurts,' she murmured, as she covered his hands with her own and urged him on. He squeezed the breasts luxuriantly, twisting them out and then in. With his forefingers he pushed each nipple into the breast, covering them with smooth flesh, and then let them spring out again. He rose on his knees and gently bit her enticing nape. Shivers ran down her spine.

The young maid entered the room bearing a tray of sweet cakes and tea. Goemon started to withdraw, but the widow pressed his hands back onto her hot tits. 'Oko, assist us please,' she said.

Without a word, the young servant approached

the couple. The widow urged Goemon on by squeezing her hands onto her breasts. He began to enjoy the game, biting her shoulders with greater fervour, thrumming nipples between his fingers. Oko quickly released his sash and drew down his trousers. She unwound his loincloth, handling his now erect prick and passing her small hands over his taut buttocks with almost disdainful coolness. Her hands still between the two moving bodies, she undid her mistress' sash and pulled it away, then opened the widow's robe. Not surprisingly, Goemon could see that the widow wore no undershirt. As the last operation was concluded, and the maid's head was close to her mistress', Goemon imagined he could hear one breathless word: 'Satisfactory,' breathed Oko.

The widow relaxed back into his arms and the maid knelt on the mat beside them. While nibbling gently on her ear, Goemon could see the length of her body. It was pleasingly smooth, and the muscular curves had barely yielded into the folds of middle age. She had a peculiarly shaped bush, long and thin, that did not cover the whole of her mons. He slid an exploratory hand downwards, past her navel where he did not linger and through the length of the hair strip. The woman shuddered when he reached the top of her cunt. She arched her body and moaned when his finger rolled over her small but wet button. He dipped lower and found the small opening awash with her juice. She moaned again.

Barely articulating her words, she murmured, 'Quickly, quickly. It's been so long now.'

He twisted his body around and allowed her to

lie flat on the floor. Oko hurriedly placed a tall wooden cushion under the nape of her mistress' head, to keep her hairdo off the ground. Goemon mounted the spread body beneath him. He stabbed with his rampant prick, but missed the opening in his excitement. His prick slid up the mossy strip, leaving a trail of wetness, his and hers. The sensation of the rough hairs smoothed by cunt juice raised Goemon's lust to a fever pitch. He tried again, and this time felt small slim hands guiding him into the widow's lustful furnace. He pushed himself all the way in. Though she was a bit loose, her overabundant moisture made up for all. Goemon felt as if he was in a pussy that he had come in already. The widow, two years of abstinence behind her, could not control herself at all, and the juicy condition of her sex evidenced her hunger.

She arched her body as he probed her inner depths. The ever-efficient Oko slipped a flat, broad sitting-cushion under her buttocks, and then knelt by their sides again. The widow then raised her legs and clasped her ankles over Goemon's back. He set to work in earnest. He clutched her ass cheeks with his hands and rammed himself furiously into the woman. She moaned with each thrust and cried out when his searching mouth clamped down on one of her nipples. He alternately bit and sucked each nipple in turn. He drove his prick far up her channel several times, and then brought it down slowly to the lips, where he played the head of his prick between the smooth lips.

'No, in, IN,' cried the widow. He obligingly thrust forth and pushed himself in as far as he could. She moaned again and then went into a perfect frenzy. Her hips beat against him, her hands moved aimlessly, and her eyes closed as if in pain. The shudders lasted for minutes, as she came seemingly without end.

Goemon had thought of keeping himself for another round, but the frenzy of the smooth body beneath him brought upon him his own climax. His balls contracted suddenly and a sticky stream emerged in giant pulses, spattering the widow's insides copiously. Flexing his powerful legs, he rammed his pole in and ground his hips into the woman's smooth thighs until she bit her lips and moaned in pain and ecstasy.

They rested for a while on the soft pallet. The widow explored every recess of Goemon's body with her fingers and tongue. She held his balls gently in the cup of her hand, tonguing each round egg gently. Goeman, his head raised on a pillow admired her touch and the elegance of her movements. His eye was caught by the immobile figure of the young maid. Her face betrayed no emotion, and her hands rested, without even a hint of pressure, on her lap.

The widow raised her eyes and caught the direction of his gaze. 'Oko, disrobe yourself,' she ordered.

The young girl rose smoothly to her feet. She undid her colourful sash and let it drop to the floor. She raised both hands to the neck of her robe, and slowly drew them down to her hips, parting the robe as she did so. The robe fell whispering to the mat floor. Her nipples were almost black. They stood up as prominent nubs over breasts that budded on her thin chest. The breasts themselves were mere swellings, hinting boldly of what was yet to come. Her face still frozen, she raised her hands to the ties of her bright red underskirt – the sole undergarment worn by women. Untying the skirt, she swayed around modestly so that her buttocks faced the pallet. Like a bird fascinated by a snake, Goemon watched the red-covered ass. She dropped the square of fabric that went around her waist twice, and Goemon could see proud tight buttocks rising above well-shaped, rather thin thighs. The vertical and horizontal creases of her ass were as clear-cut as if made by a knife. The muscles played under the pale skin as she turned around again, exposing her smooth crotch to their view. The lips of her cunt were small, covered by only the shadow of hair. She raised her hand along her body again and pulled a pin from her hair, letting a black cloud float down her shoulders. Her face still betrayed no expression.

'I can't let you have her, I'm afraid,' breathed the widow into Goemon's cupped balls. She ran her tongue up the length of his stiff prick and suckled off the drop of moisture that appeared at its tip. In a year or two I'll find her someone. In the meantime she must learn . . . Oko, come here.'

The maid approached and knelt facing her mistress. The woman dipped her head over the sack held in her palm. She gently tongued each ball again, then sucked one of them gently into her mouth. Goemon shuddered with pleasure and suppressed lust. The widow raised her head, and the young girl imitated her motions. Though she was as careful as she could be, still she was inexperi-

38

enced. Her mouth failed to bring the same sensations as that of her predecessor. The widow shook her head. 'Not yet. She still has some way to go.' She demonstrated again, and again Goemon's body shuddered. He moved his hands to touch both bodies on either side of him. The girl shook his hand off and avoided his touch. The widow tolerated it. The lesson continued.

The lesson continued higher up. The widow took the plum-shaped head of Goemon's prick between her lips. Her tongue flicked out, touching and wetting simultaneously. She yielded her position to Oko, who imitated her mistress, though with less exciting results. Goemon began appreciating his position, and he abandoned himself entirely to the women's ministrations. The widow cast him an approving glance. She moved on. Her lips touched his taut belly muscles with butterfly touches. The girl imitated her on the other side. They laved his nipples with their tongues, and nibbled up the sides of his neck to his ears. The widow changed her position. She straddled Goemon's head. Her wet cunt rubbed over his shaven forehead, then descended so that his nose was in contact with the slick soft pearl between her hairy lips. She rubbed herself on him, faster and faster, and he could barely breathe. She slapped his hands away when he reached for her, and he lay passively again. She moved forward and he licked hurriedly at her cunt.

When she dismounted, the maid took her place. She rubbed her cunt over his face. Her smoother cunt, almost hairless, dripped dew over his nose, cheeks, and jaw. He tried to lick her cunt, but the widow's slim hand intervened. Instead, the young

39

girl poised her delicate tight asshole over his face. His tongue stabbed forward and attempted to penetrate the tight ring of muscle. Again the girl was pulled away from him. She rested her mound against his forehead. As from afar, the widow's voice came to him: 'She must learn properly first, before her own pleasure.'

The widow leaned over him. Her hanging breasts tickled his chest. She drew his arms up over his head. Oko knelt with a knee on each palm. Her cunt came into full contact with his forehead, and she started liberally coating his forehead with her viriginal juices while frigging herself on the smooth expanse.

The widow looked on approvingly for a moment. With a swift movement, she mounted Goemon. Without consideration for him, she forced herself quickly down onto his rampant prick. The power of her descending body took his breath away. She rode him hard. Her hands explored his muscles, pinched and scraped his skin, squeezed his ball bags gently until he thought he was going mad.

He erupted like a volcano, spewing his milk into her waiting cunt. He felt the contractions in her insides as she bent over and bit him lovingly on the lips. With her head she nudged Oko away. Impassively, the servant girl obeyed her mistress, leaving Goemon's fragment and juice-besmeared forehead to her mistress' laving tongue.

He woke at sunset. His clothes were folded neatly at the foot of the bed. A tray held a pot of tea, some dried fish, rice, and condiment of eels. He ate it all and felt strength returning to his body. Another smaller tray held a paper-wrapped package. Intrigued at its weight, he opened the package. Folded around an oval gold coin was a paper with a quote from the 'Pillow Book' of Lady Sei Shonagon. It was signed by the impression of a cunt, made by dyeing the lips and pressing the paper to them. The mark of an erect clit made an obvious period to the affair. Goemon smiled in pleasure. She was indeed a true champion of love and, like sumo champions who stamped their handprints, needed no better signature than the one she had given. Rested, he left the house, noting as he left the device of interwined willow branches that served as the residents' badge.

CHAPTER 5

Goemon threaded his way through the streets of
Kamakura. The hills overlooking the town drew
his attention and longing. As the memory of his
encounter in town began to lose its immediacy, the
memory of the girl on the beach returned to plague
him. What was she doing here? What had happened
to her? Amazed at himself, he found that he was
wondering how she would survive, and even
considering ways to return to find her and offer her
his protection. Perhaps he, being who he was, could
do something after all.

He laughed at himself. She was leagues away, no
doubt arrested by the local authorities and on her
way to execution. He sighed, whether in frustration
or regret, he himself could not tell. The town of
Kamakura disappeared behind him. He passed a
lonely temple set well back in its tended garden.
He followed the sound of water until he came to a
small stream that ran over mossy rocks. Idly as he
walked, he drew his short sword and cut accurately
at the thin reeds that sprouted near the stream. He
came to a bamboo grove, and his sword practice
became more earnest. He had not practised for
many days, and he was dull.

He proceeded further after a while, his body pleasantly sweaty. There was a small pool, a mere widening of the stream before him. He stripped and washed. Lying in the water, he heard the sound of movement through the brush. Disdaining to dress, he drifted to his clothes and drew his sword.

An undressed figure splashed into the pool. She reflected white in the water, white topped with gold, and Goemon could hardly believe his eyes. As if in response to his call, his flaccid prick sprung erect, though the rest of him was frozen. The girl bent to splash water over herself, and her full breasts tumbled forward and swayed, kissing the water with their pink nipples. As she straightened her back she caught sight of the immobile Goemon. She recognised him at once, and the look in her eyes changed from languor to one he could not fathom. She saw his erect prick and a blush started at her face and coloured down to her heaving bosom. Her nipples, shrivelled by the cold water, became a deeper pink and started to swell. Her eyes then took in his bared sword, forgotten in his hand. She gave a shriek and turned to run.

Her movement released a spring in Goemon. 'Don't go,' he shouted at her desperately. In his confusion he shouted in Japanese. He gave chase as she scrambled through the bamboo grove.

Okiku had awakened lazily as Rosamund left her side to go and wash. She dreamily contemplated the sky, not wishing to think of their future. Finally she stripped and prepared to join Rosamund's bath. The thought of that lovely strange body brought a flush to her belly and a moistness between her thighs. Her fingers twitched as she thought of what

44

they would do during and after the bath, and as various possibilities ran through her mind.

Suddenly she heard a man call and Rosamund's panicked shriek. Without thinking, she drew her blade from its hiding place in her staff and rushed in the direction of the cries.

The man who was chasing Rosamund was naked, and his intentions were obvious from the state of his nude body. Not pausing to consider the pleading sound of his 'No, please, no, wait . . .' Okiku charged down upon him. She aimed a murderous cut at his head.

It was fortunate that Goemon's reflexes, even when concentrating on other things, were good, and his training excellent. He parried Okikù's stroke with his sword, and suddenly she was upon him. They fell to the ground, and emerged, each one holding the other's sword hand. She had a wiry strength, and had passed through a fighting school no worse than his own. The two were evenly matched. She got a purchase with one leg around his hips, and they rolled on the ground, each seeking an advantage, each fearing to let go the other's sword hand. Their bodies rubbed together. Goemon's stiff prick did not diminish. To his surprise he found the erection grow and harden. Instinctively he pushed forward. Okiku's cunt, that had been lubricated by thoughts of Rosamund, presented no barrier. Reflexively her lower mouth sucked in the morsel offered, and Goemon was in her soft canal. As their upper torsos fought and snarled at one another, their lower selves fought a battle no less serious. Goemon thrust in viciously, hoping to get his opponent to climax before he did.

45

Okiku squeezed her cunt at the moment of his withdrawing thrusts. Both knew that the first to come would be the loser: either in the throes of orgasm, or during the languor that followed, would come the other's sword stroke.

Breathing heavily, neither giving in to the other, their bodies thrust at one another. They were on their sides now, wedged between two thick bamboo trunks. They did not forget their more murderous weapons, but their thrashing did not free them. Vaguely they heard Rosamund's sobbing in the background. The movement of their hips, perhaps spurred on by the sound that meant things for both of them, quickened. The movements became shorter and harder. Their breaths hissed between bared teeth. Their breasts rose and fell, and the sweaty touch brought both of them to a climax simultaneously.

Goemon, feeling his prick begin its preliminary spurt, like a man clearing his throat before speaking, knew he was going to die. He thrust his hips out wildly, no longer caring. The intensity of the feeling overtook him as stream after stream of hot jism streaked through the channel of his prick.

Okiku could not bear the pressure any longer. Though she knew she could come again and again, she also knew that the man in her was a trained fighting man. He would seize on any moment of weakness, such as the one . . . the one . . . NOW coming. The dam in her pussy seemed to burst, as she came frenziedly. She moaned as she burst, in pleasure, in regret for Rosamund, for her own life.

Suddenly she was grabbed from behind by a large rough hand. She fell weakly on her back. Over her loomed the contorted face of the young Jiro. He drew his long sword and poised for a moment, sword over head. Goemon, knowing this was the end, stared at the glittering blade, memorising everything he saw. The glitter of light on the blade edge, the plumes of bamboo, the bared-teeth face of his executioner. His sword he knew had fallen from his hand during his climax, and he himself was trapped by the bamboo. He was ready to greet death.

'No, no!' A white nude figure interposed itself between Goemon and death. Rosamund cast herself on top of the prostrate man, shielding him from the sword. She peered fearfully over her shoulder. Her breasts, the breasts he had been longing to squeeze, to extract a pleased reaction from, pushed into his chest. He waited calmly as before.

'No? Why not? He was trying to kill Okiku!' Jiro was obviously puzzled, and he did not relax his stand.

Rosamund blushed, but answered defiantly, 'I . . . I know this man . . .'

'Know him? You had just arrived in Japan when I met you.' His voice faltered as he remembered who they met.

'Well then?! I met him the same way. On the beach, after the wreck. . . . He . . . he did what you did, and I hit him on the head to escape.' She gently touched the scab on Goemon's forehead.

'Who are you?' demanded Jiro in his gruffest voice.

Goemon rose slowly and cautiously to his feet. 'Goemon, at your service. I am a doctor.'

'And a rapist it seems,' retorted Jiro.

Rosamund snorted. She had by now learned the word. Okiku laughed slightly and Jiro had the grace to blush. The two men looked one another over cautiously. Goemon was a fine figure of a man. His frame was well knit, and his coppery skin, browned by sun, covered a rippling set of muscles. He had a finely-carved, sensitive face with mobile lips and a ready smile.

The figure he faced was almost a giant. He towered over Goemon by more than a head, with a mountainous chest. He wore the haircut and swords of a samurai, but his enormous hands looked like those of a labourer. His face though was paler than Goemon's.

Goemon broke the silence. He bowed in Rosamund's direction and said in Dutch, 'I apologise sincerely.'

'For raping me?' she said and frowned a bit.

'No. That was . . . unavoidable.' She smiled as he gestured at his prick. 'No. For not calling out in Dutch just now, so that you would not panic.'

Her face dimpled happily as she impulsively laid a hand on his shoulder. Her other hand twitched as if it too wanted to join the first one.

Goemon then bowed to Okiku. 'I apologise to you too. I am sorry our first meeting should be in this fashion.'

She laughed broadly and he flushed. 'To the contrary, doctor. I found it exciting. Dying in the midst of coming is the way I'd like to go if I must. It was new and exciting.' She made a happy sound, and laid her hand on Jiro's shoulder as he returned his sword to its sheath. 'I shall practise it again with someone else,' she added. Her hand kneaded Jiro's

48

forearm which had become stiff as an oaken branch. She laughed again, impishly.

'Jiro-san, you are too tense from your walk, and you need a bath and massage.' Her hands began undoing Jiro's clothes. Wary of Goemon's unknown intentions, he wanted to object. Rosamund, divining the problem, went to Okiku's help. They cajoled Jiro to the flat place where they had left their clothing. Rolling him on the ground with much laughing and tickling, they got him out of his clothes. Goemon followed bemusedly. The sight of Rosamund's bare ass in the fading light excited him again. He gently touched an upturned bun, and she looked at him over her shoulder with a strange expression. He squeezed harder, and she drove her ass into his palm. His naked prick thickened again, and he slid his hands down the crack of her ass until he could cup the thick-lipped, softly downed mound of her cunt. She ground her cunt into his seeking palm.

Jiro was lying on the ground, his head clutched in a neck-lock against Okiku's breast. Rosamund quickly lowered her lips. Spontaneously and for the first time, she opened her mouth and sucked at Jiro's wrinkled member. There was a momentary silence, as if a new act had started. She sucked at the large soft head, and it hardened in her mouth. Driving her head forwards, her jaws extended, she took as much of the meat into her mouth as she could, moving her tongue and wetting the length she could fit it. Jiro turned his head slightly and sucked for a moment on Okiku's pointed nipple. She thrust her breast as far as she could into his mouth and his hands sought her still-wet cunt. He parted the lips gently and inserted his finger deeply into her. Drawing the finger out, he added a second, and pressed with his thumb on the nub of her excited pink clit.

Holding his rampant prick with his left hand, Goemon parted the lips of Rosamund's cunt with his right. Slowly so as not to frighten her, he introduced his prick into the delicious folds. He pushed in gently until they were joined at the hairs. She pushed herself onto him again, and he sighed. He pulled out, and pushed in again. Her mouth was occupied, but she sent a hand between her legs to grasp his balls and urge him in. Misunderstanding, Goemon, who wanted to pound this beautiful ass before him with his body, made his movements even more gentle. She moaned in hidden disappointment. Jiro pumped his hips in her face at the feel of her throat. She felt the pain as his prick reached her glottis, and pushed it in even further.

Without allowing Jiro to let go of her nipple, Okiku twisted her body. Roughly, for she knew her power over the other girl, she shoved Rosamund away from the meat she was sucking on. Raising herself slightly, she brought herself down on Jiro's rampant prick. She was tighter and smoother than Rosamund's inexperienced mouth, and Jiro thrust into her with all the strength of his hips. She clutched at his hips and drove herself downwards. They rocked back and forth, she rising into the air as the steed beneath her arched his back while his large hands alternatively squeezed her breasts and her golden ass.

Rosamund was beginning to feel disappointed. This was the man she had dreamed of for the past three nights, and yet the meeting between them was not satisfying her. In the recesses of her mind she had imagined their meeting. This was nothing like it at all, though she could not articulate, even to herself, what was missing. Goemon continued to gently bore into her. The wiry hair at the root of his manhood scraped against her ass, and the sensation drove her mad. She ground her ass against the scraping irritation. 'Ah . . .' she whispered, then, 'Harder!' Not understanding her English, Goemon continued lightly stroking her pale smooth back.

Full of rage at the spoiling of her imaginings, she muttered again, louder this time. 'Harder, damn you.' In her frustration she stuck a hand backwards and raked her fingernails down one of his thighs. Surprised at the attack, Goemon almost yelped, and pushed at her roughly. Encouraged, she drew her nails down the same thigh. The redoubled pain made Goemon thrust into her savagely. He abandoned his smooth movements, and jerked at her as if he were trying to hook a fish. She sighed happily. Understanding began to dawn in the young doctor's mind. He slid his hands around her body and took a full teat in each hand. With a strong motion he squeezed on each breast as he pulled them down and then mashed them up against her chest. The pink nipples burned his palms. Rosamund sighed happily, and jogged her ass backwards again. He squeezed her tits roughly, and pummelled his hips at her jiggling buns. Drawing his prick almost out of her, he drove it back into her in a savage lunge. She squealed in delight and raked her fingernails over one of his hands. He pushed forward with the

51

weight of his body until she fell flat on the ground. His thighs covered hers and limited her movement while tightening the walls of her cunt. With one hand he twisted and held her hands behind her while snaking one hand between the ground and her body. There he groped at her breast, driving strong fingers into the soft mound, now mashed flat. Then he set to work to properly fuck her.

Having come once, Okiku expected to take a while to reach her climax again. She was surprised again, as she had been for the past days, by the man beneath her. His prick was large and long, and it fitted her cunt like a key to a lock. She could feel every fold of her cunt, and the bump of every vein in Jiro's manroot. He thrust into her, raising his hip into an arced bridge. He remembered arriving on the scene as Okiku and Goemon were in the throes of their orgasm, and the memory triggered a flood. Before he could think on it, he felt his prick give a twitch and he sprayed the insides of the girl with thick cream. He gave a wordless yell and his body arched further than it had so far. Above him, Okiku saw and felt his come. She tried to restrain herself, but the probing of his perfect prick sent her into paroxysms, and she fell across his chest as they spent together. They lay there for a while. She nibbled at his chest, curiously investigating the hairs that grew there profusely and enjoying the feel of his fingers working their way down the crack of her ass.

They were aroused by the sounds that came from Rosamund and Goemon. The blonde girl was stretched at full length flat on the quilt that had served as a bed. Her hands were twisted behind her, and she was sobbing, her face hidden from them. Goemon lay flat on her, one hand hidden by the curve of her body, the other holding both slim wrists. He was raising his body high, in an irregular rhythm. His long slim prick would become visible, and then he would plunge it forcefully downwards. His face was intent and he alternated bites at Rosamund's reddening back with kisses and licks of an extraordinary long and mobile tongue. As he came down, Rosamund would let out another breathless scream. Jiro, who felt protective towards the blonde castaway, began to rise in anger at the treatment she was receiving. Okiku forcefully pushed him down and restrained him. Rosamund turned her head to face them. She cried out again happily, shrilly, and they could see her climax was not far off.

Okiku grinned at the young samurai. 'She enjoys it . . .' He smiled back at her conspiratorially, stimulated by the sight, new ideas pulsing through his brain. Okiku laughed at him openly and ground her hips against him. 'Later, lover, you can try all sorts of things. Let us just watch for now.'

Goemon's whole body rose and came down on Rosamund's ass and thighs. His prick forced its way each time into her with a violent sensation. The tight friction and the sound of her moans drove him on, and his movements became more spasmodic. She urged him on, driving her tit into his hand, moving her ass to his attacks, fighting him lovingly. They both exploded together. He drove his spurting cock deep into her, and the penetration mingled with the feeling of his soothing sperm washing her insides. Rosamund's inner channel contracted forcefully, milking the spurting cock-head, and she screamed one final cry as her legs came together strongly, gripping and almost strangling his cock.

CHAPTER 6

They reached the Tokaido highway the following day. Rosamund, who had delayed them before, was now learning to keep up with the others' pace. She was now clad in a nun's habit and they felt they could risk the highway with her little Japanese.

They came upon the highway from a small road that ran along a canal embankment. To either side stretched tiny fields separated by low dykes. The highway itself was unpaved, but broad enough for four ox wagons to ride side by side. It was a constant parade of humanity, largely on foot, and their small company made not a splash. From time to time the highway passed near or through a village or small town, where vertical banners fluttered on poles announcing inns, baths, teahouses, and stables.

Jiro, as befitting a samurai retainer of the Tokugawa house, strode arrogantly along, the sight of his two swords and erect carriage cleaving a way through the traffic. Goemon walked at his side, his itinerant doctor's garb and mild manner making up for the tough appearance of his companion. The nun with downcast eyes and her accompanying pilgrim – Okiku had changed her dress, and was no longer dressed as a dancer – were obviously of the same party, and none cared to hinder them.

The country they travelled through was heavily populated. Flat land that lay between tree-covered bluffs was dyked and cut up into rice fields, some large, some minuscule. The sides of the bluffs were occupied by tiny hamlets. The houses were wooden-walled and thatched neatly. The peasants, in broad hats, worked their fields unceasingly. Ahead a range of mountains grew closer as they walked.

They slept the night in a small inn on the highway. Rosamund picked her way with difficulty through the strange foods: raw fish, boiled rice, strange-tasting pickles and soup. She took more easily to the custom of eating with chopsticks, and enjoyed dessert most of all as she happily sucked Jiro's cock to exhaustion.

They travelled in this fashion, staying at small inns, for four days. They passed the massive fortress at Odawara, and the hot springs at Atami. Eventually they rounded a bluff and Rosamund drew a breath at the full sight of something she had only had glimpses of before. A huge, perfectly conical mountain rose before them from a cinder grey plain. All three of her friends looked at her face and smiled.

'Mount Fuji: we call it Fuji-san,' said Jiro expansively as if he owned the mountain. Its truncated top glistened with snow in the clear air.

'Wonderful, isn't it?' added Okiku. 'One of the most beautiful sights in the world. It is never the same, and looks different from any angle you view it.'

There was a small shrine to Fuji-san – no more than a stone stela with some flowers before it – nearby. They approached it, bowed and clapped in respect for the mountain. Rosamund, remembering her lessons, followed suit.

Behind them a small party was just coming out of a tea house. There were two palanquins bearing the arms of a temple, and a number of monks, one of them dressed in the purple stole and high hat of an abbot. The abbot was a robust middle-aged man. He carried himself erect, and his powerful shoulders indicated that in the past he had engaged in something that required more strength than raising a prayer book. He cast a casual glance across the road and noted the party of four before the Fuji-san shrine. As he was about to enter his palanquin. Rosamund turned and looked around her. The abbot's glance sharpened as he saw the image of the nun. She was dressed in the clothes of a nun of the Zen sect, but, he decided in a flash, she was beautiful. He ran his tongue across his lips and sweat broke out on his neck. Unusually, she was made up with white powder, but the structure of the face, the round eyes, were so unusual, his decision came in a flash.

He called one of his acolytes 'Hiratsuka-san, run across and ask the nun over there if she will please accept a night's lodging at the temple.'

Jiro, who saw the monk approaching, interposed himself between the monk and the rest of the party. 'What do you want?' he asked roughly. The monk bowed.

'My master, the abbot Eiken of Fuji temple,

wishes to invite the honourable nun of your company to rest the night at our temple.'

Politely, Jiro refused. He knew that Rosamund's foreign nature would become obvious in the confines of a small monastic community: she still could not speak the language well enough, and knew nothing of monastic life. The monk tried to insist, but after Jiro refused him, he ran back to his superior. Imposingly, the abbot himself advanced upon the party. He bowed low before Jiro, who had once again interposed himself between the stranger and his friends.

'I beg leave to be allowed to invite the party of this illustrious lady to stay at the monastery. I realise the illustrious lady wishes her privacy, and I can assure her of better accommodations than will be available along the road.'

Goemon, who had been standing this while with Rosamund and Okiku a little way off, whispered urgently into Rosamund's ear, 'Call Jiro-san, quickly!'

'Jiro-san' repeated the girl in a low voice.

Jiro bowed briefly to the prelate and walked over to his friends, he bowed his ear close to Rosamund's mouth, as if listening to her instructions, while Goemon rapidly muttered, 'Take his offer. I recognise the face. He is an ex-lord, and his good will may be important to us. In any case, say that the nun wishes complete privacy, and would appreciate some transport tomorrow morning.'

Jiro bowed in acquiescence, and relayed the message to the abbot. The extra palanquin was quickly brought to Rosamund, and she settled herself uncomfortably in its confines. Okiku quickly drew the doors, while Jiro stood guard, shoulders squared. The abbot resumed his seat in his own palanquin. In the privacy of his vehicle, he smiled happily in anticipation.

They travelled rapidly across a cindery plain that rose in a smooth curve towards the foot of the mountain. Jiro strode, somewhat worried, on one side of the palanquin, Okiku and Goemon on the other.

The monastery was a large rambling structure of many interconnected wooden buildings. The two women were given a small building to themselves. It overlooked a beautifully maintained garden. The building on the other side of the garden was the abbot's own quarters, so they would be quite safe, as a verger explained to them. He was a young man and his eyes too considered Rosamund's face appreciatively. The abbot, solicitous of their well-being, sent over a local delicacy – sweet stuffed buns – which the four happily gobbled down after their simple meal. Rosamund admired the plates, the like of which she had never seen before. One, obviously her own portion, was an elaborate glazed plate shaped and woven like a basket. Those for her 'retainers' were simpler, being octagonal plates decorated with brush paintings of mountain flowers.

Still playing their parts, the women retired to bed alone on two very large pallets that had been prepared by the temple servants. Goemon had a pallet prepared in a small room nearby, whereas Jiro, as befitting his assumed position, sat himself down before the sole sliding door to the room.

In very short time, Rosamund, who had been

anticipating consoling herself with Okiku's mouth and hands, found herself the only one awake. Okiku was curled into a ball on the other pallet, snoring gently, as were Goemon and Jiro outside the room. The sounds of activity in the temple died down rapidly. Rosamund felt languid and heavy, but unable to sleep.

There was a scratching sound from the plastered wall of the room, and a hidden panel opened before her. The abbot, dressed in a light robe, stole into the room. He kneeled over Rosamund's form. She waited to see what would happen, though some corner of her mind wanted to shout in panic. She remembered gratefully that on Okiku's instructions, she had covered her hair tightly with a kerchief.

The prelate stared at her full body through the dim light cast by the candle he held. She lay there unmoving, legs slightly parted as in sleep, her perfect breasts slightly flattened by gravity. The abbot rose to his feet. His robe slipped to the floor. He had a powerful, muscular body. At the juncture of muscular thighs rose a thin, longish prick from a bed of straight hair. He flexed the muscles of his belly and the prick jerked in the air. A diamond drop formed at its tip. Rosamund, who had observed him under her lids drew in an instinctive breath of longing. He knelt quickly down and parted her legs even more.

'I know you are not asleep,' he murmured in the dark. 'Have no fear, your companions will not awake, and the drug effects will pass by the morning. You must grant me this. Seeing you at the highway, I had no choice but to have you.'

He leaned forward, and with no preliminary, shoved his prick into Rosamund. Surprisingly, he hit her hole dead centre without a fumble. Rosamund's juices had begun to flow even before he touched her. He thrust the length of his prick up her, while squatting on his heels. She sighed with pleasure. He let the length of his prick soak in her cunt for awhile while he explored her visually as well as he could. She was a large woman, which pleased him. Her face was rounded, and her lips slightly parted. It was her breasts which excited him, though. He had never seen such large ones before. Still squatting, he sent his hands forward and felt each mount with one hand. The erect nipples burned at his touch. He squeezed them lightly, then more strongly as she moved in his hands. She arched her body, and at that signal, he withdrew the length of his prick until the flange at the tip touched the full lips of her cunt. He paused for a second, then drove it hard the full length again. Rosamund arched her hips demandingly, and he repeated the motion.

Using her breasts as handles, he pulled her to him, as he repeated his long thrusts again and again. She cried softly in pleasure. Her lips parted even more, and he knew what else he would do with this delicious woman. The walls of her cunt stuck to his prick, reluctantly parting each time he thrust, sucking at him as he withdrew. His movements became quicker as his climax neared.

Roughly, he pulled at her breasts. He shook her from side to side, the weight of her shoulders and chest suspended from the two extended fruit. The pain in her breasts combined with the pleasure of the warmth of his hands. And his prick thrust its way up her length. She wanted to clamp her legs around him, but the lassitude she felt was still with her. She let him do as he would, since climax was rising through her in delicious waves. Unable to bear the pleasure any more, she bit her lip and cried again. Her hips pumped against him and her juices sped down the length of his cock. She climaxed on waves of pleasure that rose to a peak and then subsided while he roughly shook her body using his hips and the handles that her breasts provided. With one last convulsive shudder, she fell back against the bed, limp and relaxed.

The abbot withdrew his still erect prick. It glistened in the moonlight like a sword blade. Through her half-closed lids she saw the blade approach her head as he walked on his knees towards her. 'Now I will come in my turn,' he murmured at her head. Gently he pushed her over on her side and laid her head back on the high hard pillow. She relaxed and waited passively. Whatever came, she knew, would not harm her. He squatted at her head and she smelt the mixed incense of his male lust and her own juices. He leaned forward slightly, and the tip of his prick was pushing against her lips. He pushed forward and a length of his slim cock rested against her tongue. She closed her lips gently, hiding her teeth behind them so as not to bruise the morsel in her mouth. She started to suck, but his hands on her shoulder motioned her to passivity. He pushed again, and the length of his prick slid down her throat. His hair tickled her nostrils for a moment, as he rested in her mouth. Her protesting throat muscles took the opportunity to get used to the unfamiliar intruder. He withdrew then, still slowly, and stopped when only the head of his cock was between her lips. She gave a slight lick to the tip, just tasting the drop of liquid that he had emitted. In response, he shuddered and drove into her mouth again.

'I will fuck you in your mouth,' he muttered above her. 'You are very good, taking in my entire length like that.'

True to his word, he began fucking her in the mouth. His cock went its entire length and then withdrew. He rested his hands lightly on her uppermost breast, and his breath began rasping in his throat as the pleasure of this unusual channel penetrated. Rosamund sent her hand down between her legs. She grasped her prominent clitoris and began squeezing it in the same rhythm as the man's movements in her mouth. Her relaxed mouth accepted his machine without complaint and the movement of the shaft along her tongue filled her with pleasure. As he withdrew she tried to lick the moving tip. Annoyed at her interference, he slapped her tit lightly. In her mind she smiled at the added pleasure it brought, and licked again as the head was withdrawn. He slapped her breast again, harder this time. She licked again. Thinking she misunderstood his message, he pinched her nipple hard between his fingers. She whined slightly as the pain hit her, and knowing it caused more of the sensation, licked his cock again. The rhythm of his blows on her breast increased in intensity as did the movements of his cock down her throat. Convulsively she licked at the passing cock head and twisted and stroked her clit, sending questing fingers into her come-slicked hole. He slapped her breasts intending to control the situation, but the flicks of her tongue and her willing mouth-and-throat cavern proved too much for him. Jamming his cock into her face as far as it would go, the abbot felt that he burst as torrent after torrent of sticky juice spurted down her throat. Reaching her own climax, Rosamund clamped her lips around his pulsing cock just as she clamped her legs around her own questing fingers. Waves of pleasure rose and shook her body.

The abbot withdrew his drooping cock from her mouth, and she licked its length, cleaning it as it passed of every drop of come. He rested by her side for a moment.

'I am most grateful,' he whispered. 'I am sorry you must go tomorrow. In some way I feel your good deed must be reciprocated. If you wish, please feel free to apply for anything you need to the house of Sanada, where I was once known as Takehiro.' He pressed a small object into her palm, and was gone.

No one remarked on Rosamund's slight hoarseness the following morning. Before hiding her gift in her clothes, she examined it covertly. It was a tiny, exquisitely lacquered box, carved with a symbol of six coins arranged in two rows. Two loops had a cord run through them to attach to one's belt. Inside the box was a tiny scroll bearing characters she could not read. She hid the gift carefully among her clothes. For some obscure reason, she felt reluctant to explain the gift or its source.

CHAPTER 7

Bearers provided by the temple carried Rosamund
the whole of the following day. Lulled by their
peculiar smooth gait and cadence, Rosamund fell
asleep. Her companions walked beside her palanquin. She woke as they crossed a river. Gangs of
porters lolled, half naked, on a pebbly strand. As
travellers and their baggage came up, they would
hoist the traveller or his baggage indiscriminately,
and wade across the wide, shallow stream. Palanquins were borne on small rafts by several porters.
Okiku rode a porter's shoulder unselfconsciously,
and Rosamund could see her rubbing her thighs
appreciatively on the porter's muscular back.
Peeking through the slats provided in her own
closed palanquin, she admired the muscular play
on the arms of her own porters. They seemed
undernourished, but powerful shoulder muscles
writhed under their skins, and as they climbed from
the water she happily compared the muscles of their
almost naked buttocks. She wondered what those
muscles were capable of, were they driving something before them.

They bade farewell to their escort at the town of
Okitsu, on the shores of a broad bay. They found

a small inn off the highway. Their room overlooked a pleasant pine wood. Okiku was happy. She was not used to travelling this way. Her new lover was wealthy enough to stay at inns, whereas she had become accustomed to staying out in all weather, or to finding an accommodating male – not too difficult but chancy – for her use during the night.

She watched the sunset glint off Fuji-san while waiting for the massage they had ordered. The mountain never failed to intrigue and delight her, and she thought of her own mountain home. Having finished a plain meal, the four of them were relaxing on seat cushions, sipping tea. Goemon and Jiro were sprawled comfortably, their light cotton gowns open to the waist. Rosamund tried to emulate Okiku, and sat upright on her knees. She had let her hair down in the privacy of their room, and Okiku felt the need to touch the smooth, soft, blonde curls, so different from her own straight black hair. Suiting action to thought she leaned forward and touched Rosamund's hair lightly. The other girl smiled. Goemon watched them with half-closed eyelids.

Okiku rose to her feet swiftly, and pressed the blonde back into the bedding behind her. Quickly, she stripped Rosamund and herself. Goemon attempted to rise to his feet, but she quelled him with a raised hand. So deliberate were her motions that no one dared move. She spread Rosamund's legs, and then positioned her in various ways, raising her legs and then lowering them, pushing the girl's knees against her generous breasts, then slapping the rounded white buttocks until they flushed pink. She stood up and approached

Goemon, whose erection was pushing out of his robe. She flicked his cock with her fingers, and he gulped as a transparent drop flew away from the tip.

She stripped both men and made them stand side by side. Pulling them gently by their cocks, she compared them for her own and Rosamund's benefit. Jiro was the larger of the two in all aspects. He towered over Goemon, and his muscles were massive. His cock, straight and peculiarly pink in colour, was also thicker than the other's.

Goemon was slimmer, with muscles that bunched only when he moved. His skin was smooth, and unlike Jiro he was almost hairless. She turned them around, and Rosamund pleasurably examined the sight of their buttocks, recalling her thoughts of the afternoon.

Letting go of Jiro, Okiku led Goemon, still by his cock, to Rosamund, who had laid herself on her back in anticipation. In annoyance, Okiku kicked the blonde girl gently until Rosamund assumed the position on her side Okiku wanted. She pulled Goemon down and laid him so that his cock faced Rosamund's face. Leaning slightly forward, she could reach the tip with her mouth while she felt the muscles of his belly with the top of her head. From his position, Goemon could see the length of her back, with the swelling buns at their bottom.

Okiku returned quickly to Jiro and guided him to Rosamund's other end. She raised the blonde's upper leg, and pushed Jiro's head between them. He faced an erect clitoris hidden between fat smooth lips bounded with golden curls. Screwing his eyes upwards, he could see the length of Rosamund's body. Her full breasts lay one on top of the other. Goemon's legs, which he could see, were tense with anticipation.

Hurriedly, Okiku herself completed the square. Her back to Rosamund who was head to feet with her, she curved her body back while lying on her side. Goemon's head fitted between her legs, a hard comforting bulk. Before her face Jiro's prick stuck out stiffly.

They sucked and nibbled on one another for many minutes, their movements becoming faster and faster. Unable to stop themselves, the two men started coming in spurts. Annoyed, Okiku pressed her fingers hard into the base of Jiro's ball bag. His spasms diminished, but he kept on bucking into her mouth with a power she enjoyed.

Rosamund felt Goemon's starting spurts. Excited at the thought that her lover would finally come in her mouth, she pushed with her head at the erect teat, butting like a calf she had seen. Her teeth, which she had forgotten to cover in her excitement, scraped Goemon's prick painfully. His coming spurt was extinguished. Annoyed, he cuffed her shoulder. When that brought no reaction but a second butting, he pinched her shoulder hard. She squealed lightly and loosened her bite on his precious prick. She licked it carefully for awhile, and suddenly the pleasure of the situation rose in her. She was pleasuring her love in a way she had not done before, and she herself was enjoying the lingering licks and sucks of another delightful man. The thought excited her so much, her insides melted. She jerked her cunt hard against Jiro's mouth, trying to force his tongue as deep into her as his prick would have gone. Divining her desire, Jiro rammed his tongue deeply into her sweet hole, tasting her musky salty insides, and sucking her soft lips as he did so. Her climax rose like a storm, and she covered Jiro's mouth and tongue with her juices.

At the same time Jiro, who felt her coming, began desperately ramming into Okiku's mouth. She held his muscular ass in both arms and encouraged him into her. With the first spurts of pearly come, she felt her own insides erupting. Her juices covered Goemon's face as he frantically achieved his own climax, spurting a heavy load of come into Rosamund's welcoming mouth.

'Excuse me. The masseuse is here.' A voice from the small ante-room broke into the fog of their lust. Goemon, writhing in orgasm, could only gasp as Okiku's lower lips filled his mouth. Jiro was in no better shape. Okiku removed her mouth from Jiro's emptying prick, swallowed the come in her mouth and called out sweetly, 'Please come in.' The other three froze. Goemon restrained his twitching hips as the last of his come was swallowed by Rosamund.

The masseuse came in and paused by the sliding door. She bowed, but her face showed no emotion at the four bodies on the floor.

'Over here, please,' Okiku directed her. Okiku laughed at her companions' shock. 'Blind,' she pantomimed with her hands. All masseuses were blind. That and lute playing were by tradition reserved for the blind alone. Goemon, who had forgotten, and Jiro and Rosamund, who had not known, relaxed.

'Who's first?' asked Okiku lightly. Jiro and

Goemon deferred to one another for a moment, until Okiku firmly pushed Jiro down on his stomach, and led the masseuse over to him. The masseuse was a muscular woman dressed in a plain robe. She had a pleasant face, but for her vacant staring eyes. She squatted before Jiro's supine body and began pressing and kneading his back, her dead eyes staring at nothing.

Okiku calmly pushed Goemon down as well. As the masseuse worked, she idly played with the man's flaccid prick. Rosamund looked at the sight for a moment, and then joined her friend on the man's other side. Occasionally, one of them would bend down and kiss the prick's tip. Goemon stretched out his hands, intending to run them along Rosamund's breasts. Okiku would have none of that. She firmly pulled the hand on her side down and sat on it. Rosamund saw her rocking slowly and copied the motion. They slid their cunts up and down the man's muscular forearms, while diddling him together.

The masseuse ordered Jiro to turn around so she could work on his legs and thighs. Suddenly he saw what his friends were about. His prick thickened and climbed into the air. The masseuse, bending over him, accidently came into contact with his tool. She gave no sign of noticing but went on with her task. Jiro was about to reach for her, but was dissuaded by Okiku's menacing hiss and glance.

The two girls rode Goemon's forearms. They stopped massaging his rampant weapon every time it threatened to explode. They smoothed the muscles of his belly, and Rosamund twitched the hairs below it, pulling them painfully. Goemon's sensitive face contorted with lust and frustration.

The masseuse finished with Jiro and the two girls rolled Goemon on his face. As the masseuse worked over the slimmer man, the two girls repeated their previous actions with Jiro. Okiku introduced a new element: she slapped Jiro's erect prick, and it swayed towards Rosamund. Laughing, she hit it back. Jiro groaned with excitement. Later Rosamund introduced a refinement and hit the erect prick with her full pendant breast. Jiro smiled at her gratefully, and Okiku slid back, resting her cunt on his fingers. He dug into the soft folds almost savagely, Okiku began to come. Rosamund followed suit, and the two girls bucked and shook over Jiro's clutching and probing fingers, their lips meeting one another's, and then Jiro's, in a double, then triple kiss.

The masseuse worked over Goemon's taut buttocks. Strands of hair had fallen from her hairdo and tickled his skin. She did not bother to move them. As her strong fingers dug into the hard muscles of his ass, the sweat ran down her back. With an easy motion she dropped the robe from her torso, uncovering a muscled back and two pear-shaped, dark-tipped breasts. Goemon rammed his frustrated member into the pallet beneath him as the masseuse continued her probing.

Finishing with his back, she rolled the young man over, and started with his thighs. Goemon's breathing became harsh, his eyes stared from his head and his face twisted. His cock was red and angry, the flanged head staring upwards and outwards. His hands crooked like claws and he dug

71

them into the masseuse's slim hips. Okiku leaped from her seat on Jiro's hand, her cunt streaming juices down her thighs, and stripped the gown and red underskirt from the masseuse's body. Goemon drew the masseuse up by main force and held her cunt over the tip of his erect maleness. The tip searched between the lush hair growth until Goemon was certain he was nestling between the lips in the right position. Lowering his hands, still clawing at her hips, he brought her to him. The slap of their two bodies was more than Jiro could bear, and he rose and shook Rosamund off, a wild look on his face. The masseuse dug her fingers into Goemon's chest as she continued her work, though her movements were less sure and more convulsive than before. Her blind face still betrayed no emotion.

Okiku turned and motioned to Jiro. She bent over the sweating girl who had straddled Goemon, moving her hips up and down his cock as she dug her fingers into his chest and the muscles of his side. Okiku sent her fingers from Goemon's cock, rooted in juice, up the crack of the other woman's ass. She found the small clenched hole of her anus. Using cunt juice, she lubricated the hole copiously, and then drove her slim finger up the masseuse's ass. The clenched muscles relaxed and she drew her finger out slowly, shoving in another one as soon as she could. The masseuse started a slow humming sound in her throat. She drove her hips harder than her fingers, and drops of hot sweat spattered Goemon beneath her. Okiku added another two fingers, and the fucked girl hummed louder and stuck her ass into the air. Jiro, tempted beyond reason, shoved Okiku aside. He kneeled between Goemon's legs and probed the masseuse's slim ass. The enormous head of his cock parted the brown half moons, and the girl gave an anticipatory shudder. Jiro pushed forward, and the masseuse cried out in joy before he was halfway there. Jiro pulled himself slowly out to the head, then again, he thrust in, and once again. The masseuse did not stop working the while. Occasionally, she would give a shudder. Aside from her shudders, and working arms and fingers, she seemed oblivious to what was being done to her.

The two vigorous young men pushed together, suiting their movements to one another. Suddenly the woman between them gave a massive shudder and came. She sighed happily, and continued her work. Held between the two men, she was entirely dependent on their movement for her pleasure. Happily for her, having come just a short while before, they were as prepared to go on as she. Relaxed, she waited for another orgasm. In her spasms, she raised her head, staring with blind eyes at the ceiling, perhaps at the gods who had afforded her such pleasure.

Okiku motioned Rosamund over to her. The blonde girl stood, straddling Goemon, and presented her cunt, still dewy with her come, to the masseuse. The blind girl had finished kneading Goemon's muscles, and she began on her new client. She gently wet the insides of the blonde's thighs with her tongue, and then dug her fingers into the magnificent thighs. The inner part of each thigh came first, then the lips between them. When Rosamund began jerking in passion, she moved to

73

the blonde's curved belly. Then, at Okiku's whispered suggestion, she had the blonde turn around. She licked the smooth expanse of the girl's ass, then separated the buttocks and sent a tongue messenger into the clenched muscular bud. The tongue was soon replaced by strong fingers, and Rosamund shuddered again as she achieved another climax. The smooth probing did not stop. Okiku now made Rosamund kneel over Goemon's mouth.

He commenced tonguing her happily. She tasted different from Okiku, with a stronger, earthier scent. The masseuse continued her work, her hands now kneading Rosamund's back, but her tongue met Goemon's occasionally, in between smoothing and pleasuring Rosamund's asshole, now completely relaxed.

Okiku paused to examine her handiwork. Concerned then with her own pleasure, she straddled the masseuse's body and pulled Jiro's head to her. He eagerly stuck his tongue into her wet twat. She held his hands and led them to her breasts that were aching with desire, their nipples erect. She fumbled behind her and found Goemon's hands, still crooked into the masseuse's hips. He raised one of his hands and dug into her slim buttock then, at her urging, drove one finger into her ass, and she rode tongue and finger to her climax. The last sight she saw before orgasm took them all was her perfect mountain of pleasure, with her at the top, and she smiled at the thought of achieving Buddhist paradise while still in life.

They came like an avalanche. The masseuse collapsed first, the throes of her coming racking her body. Okiku and Jiro fell on top of her, and

Rosamund, cramped in her kneeling position, stretched out her legs as the final shudders took her. Goemon, bearing the weight of four bodies, shook them off, laughing as soon as he got his breath back. They lay there for some time, panting and idly fingering one another until Okiku rose to offer them more tea.

Their road took them now between flat rice fields, now up or down the slopes of steep hillsides. The travellers they met or passed on the road were generally common people. Craftsmen hurrying to an assignment, an occasional messenger riding a rare horse, priests and pilgrims. They kept to themselves, sleeping in available inns or sometimes in the fields.

After several days' walking they reached the broad valley of the Tenryu river. Coiling like a dragon it wended its way to the sea from the high blue mountains to the north. Goemon, who was walking slightly behind, having treated a patient with a hurt foot, heard the sound first. He hurried up to Jiro.

'Listen!'

Jiro cupped a hand to his ear, then looked around for a place to stop. Behind them they could see a column of dust. The road ran here on a raised dyke and offered no shelter. They hurried ahead to a small hamlet that bordered the highway, and Jiro hustled them off the road.

The parade was upon them before they could enter the hamlet or find an inn. Jiro, Okiku, and Goemon hastily knelt at the side of the highway.

'Kneel quickly, bow your head, and don't move

until I tell you to,' Jiro ordered Rosamund fiercely. Her companions had all knelt, the two commoners with their faces to the dust, Jiro with his head slightly raised, his hands prominently on the ground before him. Twisting her face slightly, Rosamund watched the parade pass before her.

It made a brave sight. First came two men carrying large red boxes over poles on their shoulders. They were followed by a company of lancers, then a company of bowmen, and one of musketeers. A single rider followed, shaded by a red umbrella. He was a fierce, moustached old man, who peered keenly around him. He was followed by a group of functionaries bearing personal possessions in large wicker hampers. Then came another company of lancers. Ten men bearing poles topped with horse-hair fringes, a man carrying a folded umbrella encased in cock's feathers, followed. Then another single rider, dressed in gold-embroidered clothes and shaded by a red umbrella. This one was surrounded by high-class samurai in loose split trousers and lacquered hats. Rosamund caught a sight of his face. Young and dissipated looking, it was disfigured by several bold scars. Several more troops of infantry closed up the parade.

After the last of the parade had passed, Jiro motioned them to raise their heads. Rosamund breathed deeply. Her legs were badly cramped and her knees hurt abominably. Goemon motioned her to sit, and massaged her sore legs. The few people who had, like them, bowed before the parade, went off about their business, and Goemon risked a quick pinch at Rosamund's covered mound. She chuckled, and her thoughts returned from the magnificence of the parade.

'Was that not the king of Japan?' she asked in awe.

Jiro laughed. 'No, that was only a minor baron.'

'Minor? Riding in such splendour?' She had once seen the parade of the Infante, son of the king of Spain, and it had been far less elaborate and rich than the parade she had just seen.

'A very minor baron, the smallest there is,' said Goemon roughly. There was a strange catch in his throat. 'Did you see those fringed poles? They indicate his wealth. A mere ten-thousand koku. A koku is a measure of rice, and ten-thousand is the SMALLEST possible fief for a baron. I've . . . I've seen much larger ones, and so no doubt has Jiro. And they didn't march too well either.'

Jiro gave him a sharp glance, and as they walked, the two young men discussed the merits of the various marching fashions: raised foot, crow's walk, strut. To Jiro's surprise, Goemon was more knowledgeable than an itinerant doctor should be. Over their shoulders, black clouds gathered over the peaks of the mountain range, but in the broad plain they walked in warm sunlight.

CHAPTER 8

The Tenryu river was the broadest they had come to so far. The crossing was in stages, as sandbars striped the surface of the waters. Rosamund was again thrilled at the sight of the muscular porters, some adorned with boldly coloured tattoos. She and Okiku were seated on flat board palanquins that were carried across low fords, and floated through the deeper parts. Jiro and Goemon waded across or rode the shoulders of a porter. They were the last travellers of the day, as the sun was close to the horizon. The porters, tired from having ferried the baron's retinue, talked little.

The sun in their eyes and their tiredness made the porters less cautious than they would have been normally. The sudden rainfall had swelled the rivers in the far mountains to the north. Waves roiled the normally placid surfaces of many streams as they poured themselves, chuckling, into larger rivers. The water rushed through the deep channels of the mountain gorges, carrying branches, grass, leaves, and the occasional living thing.

Japan is a land of earthquakes, and an earthquake strikes some area in the islands every day. Most of them are minor. As the porters took a deep breath and started across the final portion of the river, a slightly larger earthquake shook the bed of the river. The tired porters tried to keep their balance on the shifting and treacherous pebbles, now turned to living moving things. They failed, and as they struggled, the entire party was hit by a wave from the rainfloods.

Goemon, riding the shoulders of a burly porter, was the first to notice the charging wave. His porter was distracted by his cry, and could no longer keep his balance. Both men tumbled into the water. Jiro, who had been walking across by himself, turned to help his friend and was struck behind by a heavy branch that tobogganed the top of the wave. Porters and board palanquins were separated, spun around and swept apart. Both girls clung desperately to their rafts. Rosamund, being heavier and clumsier, upset her raft after a few turns, and the last Okiku saw of her was the glint of damp gold as she was swallowed by a wave. She lay flat on the board paddling desperately towards a dimly-seen shore, as darkness and rain fell simultaneously.

Rosamund awoke to the sound of cheerful voices somewhere near her. She panicked for a moment, imagining she had returned to the sodden beach after her shipwreck. Listening carefully though, she could understand what was being said. There was a fire burning not far from where she lay on the bank. She shivered in her sodden robes and retched the river water. A man who had been standing with his back to the fire cocked his head. In fear of discovery, she tried crawling backwards, and fell into the water again. The man bounded forward with a yell of surprise, and rough hands helped her out of the water and laid her on a rough grass mat near the fire. She revived to the feel of some fiery rough liquid being forced between her teeth. She coughed and spluttered and opened her eyes.

She was lying in a small open shack, facing a fire. Beyond the fire she could hear the sound of the still roiling river. She studied her saviours or captors for a moment. There were six of them. Most had badly shaven foreheads, and their topknots, unlike those of Jiro and Goemon, were scruffy and unkempt. They all wore loincloths that pouched their balls and cocks, leaving little to the imagination. Most of them were tattooed in brilliant colours and intricate patters. The firelight played on their skins, and Rosamund admired their muscles that bunched the skin on their stocky frames. One of them, taller than the rest and the only one that wore a short, open jacket, rose from his kneeling position by her.

'A Southern Barbarian woman,' he said in a strong country accent. He turned to look at her and ran his tongue across his lips. The other men devoured her with their eyes, and Rosamund suddenly noticed she was naked. She sat up and tried to cover her generous breasts that bounced at her movement. The men stirred uneasily.

'I have never seen such a one before,' one of the men, almost a youth, said.

Another swayed closer and cleared a dry throat, 'Nor touched . . .' The six of them shifted as a grove of trees does before a storm. Their eyes glowed and their breathing became hoarse. Knowing what was in store for her from these men,

81

Rosamund turned to run. The men surged forward. Rough hands grabbed parts of her anatomy. A foot tripped her and she fell to the floor face-first, bouncing painfully on her full breasts. A hand pulled her hair. Another got a grip on her thigh, and a third hooked painful fingers in her dry pussy. She screamed as she was covered by a pile of lust-filled bodies that stabbed at her from every direction with blunt fleshy swords.

'Stop!' The tall, jacketed man roared at his companions. He cuffed them roughly aside and stood with his hands on his hips looking at the cowering girl. She faced him trembling, her hands crooked into claws. He grinned and called out something to his companions. Two of them scampered off into the dark. Rosamund's fear increased. They were going to fetch the authorities, and she would be killed. The two men reappeared almost immediately with some poles used for the palanquins they used to ferry travellers. The other four surrounded Rosamund purposively.

While the first two hastily improvised a wooden framework, the other four overcame the struggling girl. They lashed her to the framework. Rosamund had had occasion before to see how dexterous the Japanese were at tying complicated and elegant knots, and while she tried to twist herself free, she knew with a sick certainty what the next act of the drama would be.

She felt her bonds. A pole ran under her shoulders and her hands were tied to its ends. Three other poles formed a rough triangle with her head at the apex and her feet tied to the angles. She breathed deeply, in terror mixed with expectancy as she saw the effect her posture had on the men.

Stripped of their loincloths they were playing a quick finger game. The leader did not participate. He stood between her outstretched legs, admiring the full curves of her body. His slightly curved cock jutted from a muscular belly, and he flexed the muscles of his thighs in anticipation. Beads of sweat stood out from the stubble on his roughly shaven forehead. Finally he fell on his knees between Rosamund's outstretched legs. With the two fingers of his left hand he separated the generous lips of her cunt. With the other hand he pointed the tip of his cock into the exposed hole. With a cry he forced himself into her to the root, and fell flat onto her pale body. He closed his teeth roughly on one of her pink prominent nipples, goosebumped from the cold.

Rosamund cried out as the combined assaults of his cock, weight, and teeth made themselves felt. She was dry as he entered and his rough cock scraped her insides with an intensity she was not used to. She tried to buck him off, but the thrust of her hips only excited him more. He drew himself partly out, changed his teeth to the other nipple and thrust himself home again. She shrieked at the assault and moved herself again. He followed her with punishing blows. She closed her eyes, to hide her shame and fear. The familiar darkness made the feel of his cock more familiar. Her insides reacted instinctively. Her generous cunt oozed its gifts, lubricating the length of the shaft that was pummelling it. Her breasts swelled and her nipples, excited at the rough feel of the teeth, grew full and firm.

She breathed again, but with greater ease. He did not slacken his efforts, and they began pleasing her more and more. She could do nothing to aid this man inside her, and she surrendered therefore to her own pleasure.

Suddenly he tensed. His pushes became more rapid. He gave a cry and his teeth clenched on her nipple, bringing blood. All too soon her insides were showered with his generous come. Surprised, she opened her eyes. He was lying there motionless, his face pillowed between her breasts. She twitched her hips a bit, and he slid slimily out of her. She glared at him in frustration and annoyance.

The others urged him off. A thin man with a stubby cock took his place. This one was as hurried as the first. He plunged his cock into her thirsty slick pussy as rapidly as he could. Before she could begin to feel, he clutched her generous buns with hard strong fingers and his cock spat out its load. He rested on her breast, panting for a while, his eyes closed. A Third kicked him and he reluctantly rose, shielding his shrunken manhood from sight with his hand.

The one who entered her now was in a frenzy of lust. He opened her unnecessarily wide with blunt probing fingers. She barely had time to see the shape of his cock, rising from a thick tangle of black hair, before he had laid himself on her and shoved himself forward. This time she was deter-mined to enjoy the sensation as much as he. Remembering Okiku's ability, she contracted her cunt forcefully around the probing member. The porter groaned with lust as he forced himself further into the suddenly constricted tunnel. He

84

pulled out in the return stroke, and Rosamund tried to hold him in, but her lack of practice and the slickness of her channel did not allow her to hold him.

Before she had a chance to rest, another man knelt between her legs. He was a young man, practically a boy. His shoulders were the widest Rosamund had ever seen on a youngster. He held his cock with his hand as if to shield it from her gaze, and his eyes roved over her body, refusing to meet hers. Sweat was beading his brow. He was nervous, she realised. He stabbed at her hungry opening several times. His tip brushed against her clitoris and she sighed with anticipation. He stabbed again, higher this time, almost sobbing with frustration. The other men looked on, and joked among themselves in a rough cant she couldn't follow. 'Why, it's his first time!' she suddenly realised. She smiled at him, to encourage him. He half smiled back, then as if afraid of his temerity, scowled at her. She shifted her hips trying to help him. At last the tip of his tool found the gluey opening. He rammed himself inside and began a rapid motion in and out of her sopping cunt, as if he couldn't wait to savour the pleasure. She tried to slow him down, to encourage him by guiding his motions with her hips and cunt. Goaded by his friends' sarcastic comments he simply dug into her quicker and harder, his hands clutching her tits painfully but ineffectually as she got little pleasure from him.

He screamed loudly as he came, grinding rough hips into the bowl of her legs. She felt the warm spurts inundate her insides, but again, the event was over too quickly before she could enjoy her feelings to the fullest. She was now in an agony of lust and twisted her body hopefully as the young man withdrew. Notwithstanding his disappointing performance, she smiled at him as he withdrew. This time he smiled too, in what he thought was his moment of triumph. Rosamund felt sorry for him for a fleeting moment, so young, and unable to satisfy her.

The leader noted her smile and the writhing of her hips. He knelt by her head and took her chin roughly in his hands.

'You like us, hey? Well, you'll get plenty of us. And maybe we can get something else out of you before we sell you to a house.' He laughed. Rosamund did not answer, and made no sign she had understood his Japanese at all. 'My name is Ichiro. I am number one in this gang.' He thumped his chest. 'You'll learn Japanese and be a good little whore.' He laughed again, and continued holding her chin as the last two of his companions entered her one after the other. They were as quick as the rest, and when they had left her, she sighed again in frustration, and thought longingly of her lost lovers.

The men kept her tied the rest of the night. Occasionally one of them would mount her without ceremony, buck inside her for a few short moments, and then come before she had reached satisfaction. Ichiro watched her with amusement.

'You want to come, don't you, little flower? I will make you.'

She pretended not to understand. This time he stayed on her for a longer period. His hands roughly forced their way into every recess of her body. He shoved two fingers up her ass, then added a finger to his plunging cock. He was pleasingly rough, and Rosamund felt herself tense as she readied to come. Then she caught the look in his eyes. He was waiting expectantly for her climax. For him, the pleasure was in the triumph over her surrender. Bodily pleasure was secondary. A feeling of rebellion rose in her mind. She had learned to love her body, to enjoy the harsh and soft sensations of a person enjoying it, but it was the delight of mutual pleasure that she loved, and she would not be this uncouth labourer's plaything. She squeezed her cunt walls trying to squeeze him out. Her sudden movement and the resolution in her eyes caused Ichiro to lose his own control. He slapped her tit as he withdrew from her and went to join the men who were gambling at the other side of the room. He looked at her thoughtfully over his shoulder, as if checking to see that she had actually defied his intentions. She met his gaze forcefully, and it was he, not she, who lowered his eyes. She resolved that come what may, she would beat this man. She would take whatever pleasure they gave, but it would be she who would eventually dictate the pace.

The men went out in the morning to their work. She was untied from the frame, then tied again with her hands behind her back and a gag in her mouth. They fed her in the morning and again in the evening and after darkness had fallen: a stew of fish, rice, and vegetables.

She was tied again to the frame, though she fought them with all her strength, and scratched

87

the young boy who was incautious enough to come under her hands.

Ichiro, who had not participated in the struggle, laughed at his minions. 'A flower with thorns eh?' He looked at her prone body thoughtfully as he loosened his loincloth.

'Have you called the other gangs?' he asked over his shoulder as he forced his way into her dry cunt with a shove. The penetration of his prick and the heat caused by the friction of his movement caused a burning sensation in Rosamund's pussy. Then her nature took its course and her inside channel was flooded by her sweet secretions.

'Yes,' one of the men answered. 'They'll be here well after dark.'

'Good,' grunted Ichiro, his attention only half on her. 'See that there is complete darkness. I don't want them to see what kind of woman she is. If rumours got around that we have a Southern Barbarian woman here, the authorities would be here in nothing flat, and we would end with our heads on spikes.'

The inside of the hut was pitch black by the time the men had all had their turn in her soft and now gluey cunt. Her ass was resting in drips of come. There were rustlings and the sound of men talking and laughing in low voices outside the hut. Ichiro bent over her.

'Well, little flower. Your time has come. You will be able to help us poor porters a bit. Ichiro's gang will be rich by the end of the night.' He quickly gagged her with a cloth strip, and squatted by her head.

'Send the first one in, ' he ordered.

Rosamund didn't bother counting the men who mounted her helpless body that night. They were almost uniform in their strong hurried thrusts. She imagined the powerful asses and thighs that drove the cocks deep into her, bringing herself close to climax. Each time she almost reached her peak, she recalled the sardonic look of the man who squatted by her her head and controlled the gang rape, and controlled herself.

She wondered abstractedly at how unimaginative the men were. She had, she knew lovely tits, a mouth, an asshole, hands, and yet all they could think of was to plunk themselves down between her spread legs, thrust themselves in a couple of times, and collapse in an agony of simple pleasure. She giggled at the thought, and though the gag stifled the sound, Ichiro beside her moved in surprise and unease.

She played games, using whatever freedom the frame allowed her. She felt the hard muscles between her legs with her thighs, comparing size and hardness. Remembering Okiku (and almost crying with longing as a consequence) she tried constricting the muscles of her sheath over the cocks that rode in it. As the night wore on, her muscles reacted more and more to her commands, and she amused herself by trying to force the men to come at her whim.

She fell asleep once the last man had left her. She awoke in a drying pool of come, and was allowed to wash. One of the men approached her incautiously, fascinated by her full dangling breasts, and she stabbed at him with a backbrush hanging near the barrel. He doubled over in pain and his friends laughed.

Ichiro regarded her with annoyance as she was tied up again. She looked as fresh as the flower he had named her for. By now the duel between them should have been over, with her a sodden crying wreck. Well, a few more days. He jingled the coins in his sleeve contentedly.

The night was a repetition of the previous one. She could distinguish the sound of copper as money changed hands. The same boring pricks rode up her cunt again, and she could feel the pool of come beneath her ass spread in the damp sticky puddle. She played her game again, squeezing pricks with all her might. The line was longer this night; the news had spread to all the porter gangs in the area.

By the end of the evening, Rosamund had full control of the men in her. She would feel the thighs with her own. If they pleased her – firm, smooth – she would assist in the action. She would move her hips in a round motion calculated to touch the prick at its most sensitive part. If the man responded the way she wished – feeling her tits and pinching the erect nipples, cupping her ass and running slick hands over her hips and shoulders – she would continue the treatment. She found she could relax or tighten the muscles of her cunt at will, making men groan in pleasure at the tightness, or fight frantically to dig into her, searching for some opposing pleasure.

Under her ministrations, the men came as and when she wanted them to. She held on to one finely muscled body for so long, Ichiro barked at him to hurry, and even then she only relented to let the poor soul have his fill when Ichiro threatened to pull him off her. Most she finished with a few short smooth clenchings of her internal muscles.

She was spread out again that night. Ichiro clenched his jaw. She looked again a picture of freshness, notwithstanding having satisfied close to a hundred men. He wondered what would cause her to lose control. There would be no crowd this evening. Someone had talked, and a runner from the magistrate's court had been seen sniffing around. They would have to keep her privately for awhile, and then move her on to a house.

He took out his cock and advanced on the helpless girl. She met his gaze steadily, and then smiled. Enraged, he bent and slapped her tits. She smiled again, wider this time. Ichiro almost went berserk. He was about to smash his full fist into her face, when the thought of her value stopped him. He looked at her perfect pale body for a moment. The thought of her future brought a smile to his lips.

'I'm going to sell you, little flower,' he hissed. 'But before I do, I'll mark you as my property.' He pinched her thigh painfully and smiled. 'Fetch Sunekichi!' he ordered.

'The tattooist?' one of his men inquired in surprise.

'Of course, you idiot. We have to get rid of her now that the runners have got wind of her existence, but she has to be tattooed first, so she'll be saleable as a whore.'

The man scampered off and returned after a while. With him was a small, fussy old man. His topknot was shinily erect and his pate smoothly shaven. He carried a bundle wrapped in a blue dyed kerchief.

He looked at her thoughtfully for awhile once Ichiro had explained what he wanted.

'Yes, yes,' he sighed happily in a creaky voice. 'One doesn't often get to work on such magnificent skin. I'll make a masterpiece . . .

He extracted several small pots of pigment and a comblike instrument with four sharp metal teeth. Before starting he turned to Ichiro. 'Part of my fee will be the pleasuring of this flower of yours.'

Ichiro smiled and bowed. The old man squatted between her legs and regarded her body thoughtfully. Then, preparing his pigments he set to work.

She gasped when she felt the tattooing comb bite into the flesh of her inner thigh. Tiny spots of blood oozed out and stood like rich lacquer on the pale-white skin. The little man chuckled and drove the comb in again, then paused to wipe off the oozing droplets of blood. She quivered at the touch, and he eyed her thoughtfully. He dipped the comb into pigment and drove it again into her thigh. The pain in such a sensitive spot made her hiss as she expelled her breath. Quickly and steadily he elaborated a multi-coloured image on her skin. Holding her hip with one hand, he worked for a few minutes on the outer lip of cunt. The pleasurable biting pain was almost more than she could bear, and she moaned and twitched her hips until he slapped her sharply.

This time, instead of reaching for the sheet of soft paper he had used to wipe her before, Sune-kichi leaned forward and licked the inside of her thigh. Looking down the length of her body, Rosamund could see that the old skinny man had an incredible length of tongue. He delicately touched each droplet of blood, and then with a flick, he laved the length of her cunt. Though she was expecting it, Rosamund jumped. The burning pain in the inside of her thigh and cunt lips was transformed to a living thing that threatened to consume the lower parts of her body.

She steeled herself and strengthened her resolve. So far, she had beaten her captors and they cowered before her. She had taken all they had had to give and had not been bowed. She would not surrender this time, though, since she had by now discovered about herself, pain and sex were irresistible. Sunekichi bent once again to his task. Again he applied the punch, and again bent his head to clean away the blood. She barely moved this time, just smiled happily even though his tongue lingered for awhile on her clit, which stood out like a beckoning fleshy claw.

The last line was drawn and filled in. Rosamund was in a frenzy of impatience. The burning in her thigh had transferred wholly to her sex, and she knew that she needed relief, and she needed it now. Had Ichiro but known, he could have broken her on the spot. Her need threatened to engulf her. Sunekichi the tattooist rose and stripped off his loincloth. His small stringy body was complemented by a small cock, quivering erect.

He stretched out on her expectant body and drove himself deep into her. She groaned and urged him on. The friction against the pinpricks in her thigh and cunt lips made her wild. Her hips gyrated uncontrollably. Sunekichi rode her wildness for awhile. He gazed into her face, then lowered his lips to her cherry-tipped tits. The thought of the work he would do in the days to come drove him on in a frenzy.

Sunekichi groaned as his come left him in an unstoppable stream. He had creamed before she was ready, and in anger she applied the muscles of her now well-practiced twat. She squeezed his tool unmercifully, and he cried out once again. The watching porters could not understand the noises he was making, and they crowded closer to see the end of the drama. She squeezed harder and Sunekichi howled in earnest. His prick, particularly sensitive after having come, was being squeezed to death by the girl lying under him. Panic rose in his mind. He remembered the stories he had heard in his childhood about the foreign devils and their strange ways. He knew that this stranger, on whom he had expended so much living effort, was out to kill him at the core of his being. The porters, sensing the little man was in some sort of difficulty with their woman, laughed uproariously.

'I'll teach you, you little rabbit!' Rosamund screamed between clenched teeth. The porters laughed louder.

'No, no!' he howled. He felt around him for something that would help him out of his predicament. He pummelled her breasts with gnarled fingers and Rosamund smiled terribly. The pain strengthed her resolve. He would have reached for her eyes, but their intense blue, concentrated in a baleful glare, scared him. He lowered one hand and beat at an exposed hip. She screamed with pleasure. One of the laughing porters knelt for a moment. She felt the ties that had bound her ankles fall away. Her muscles were wooden from being tied too long, but with an effort she raised her legs and flung them over Sunekichi's back. Her beautiful legs clasped the little man to her. Ichiro, the leader, bent over to see the sight and noticed her tight brownish asshole. He smiled and inserted a finger, which was clasped tightly by her rear. Gently, and then roughly, he pushed it in and out, raising his head to watch her face. She was smiling beatifically at the tattooist's panic-stricken face. The finger in her sensitive rectum, and the power she felt over the man lying on her, combined in her senses. She came explosively, clenching asshole and cunt and legs in a momentous spasm. Ichiro felt the strong muscles of her asshole tighten about his finger. The muscles of her cunt and thighs tightened too. Sunekichi screamed in pain and fear. Rosamund screamed loud in triumph just as the small man's searching hand closed on his tatooing comb. He raised his hand and his body arched upward, preparatory to bringing the toothed comb down on her exposed throat, where he could gouge and twist to her lifeblood.

There was a sudden hissing, humming sound. The sole candle that had illuminated the scene went out as a whirling *shaken* hit it and cut off the tip. In the darkness, before the group of men that surrounded her could begin to cry out. Rosamund heard another humming whisper. Something heavy fell and rolled over her clenched legs. A sudden fountain of some warm sticky liquid sprayed over her. Sunekichi's body toppled to lie on her breast, his headless neck pumping blood. She screamed in panic and almost choked on his blood. She wriggled her body as well as she could and the pumping carcass fell off to one side.

Around her she could hear occasional screams. There were cries of 'Light! Light!' and 'What's going on?' which were followed soon by an ominous silence. In panic and shock, her victory snatched from her, Rosamund sobbed silently in the dark.

CHAPTER 9

Pulling herself from the water was not difficult for the athletic Okiku. The dark obscured the river. She ran upstream, calling names, hoping against hope that someone had survived the sudden flood. The river rolled on, roiled by waves and uncaring as she called out.

'Jiro, Jirooooo!! Goemon! Where are you!' She was almost crazed with grief. For a second time she had lost those dear to her. Only a natural caution stopped her from calling out Rosamund's name.

She walked the river bank for the rest of the night. She found flotsam littering the pebbly river bank, and her heart jumped once or twice at the sight of bodies. Nothing, not even the bodies, was familiar. She reached the highway again by daybreak. The rough waves on the river were abating. Still she searched, asking people whether they had seen any of her companions. There were many bodies cast out by the river that day, but none of them were known to her.

As evening fell she found a small grove surrounding a shrine just off the highway. She curled herself up for sleep, rocking herself in grief that had been abated during the day by hope.

She fell off into a doze. In a half-dream she imagined she could hear Jiro's voice. He was walking towards her, still invisible. As he approached in her dream, his voice changed. Its timbre grew higher and it assumed hateful characteristics. Suddenly Hachiro stood before her, laughing again. The dream irises dropped from her dream hands and she launched herself at the hateful face. Hachiro kept on singing a ribald song about a girl from Miyako, and he drifted away from her, his voice dwindling.

Suddenly she was awake. The voice she heard dwindling in the distance was real, not a dream. The huntress in her awoke again, after many days of soft loving. She tied her straw sandals hurriedly and raced out into the road. The singing disappeared in the distance, and she ran after it, her hand clutching her staff.

She ran for several miles, but the sound did not repeat itself. Panting, she stopped at a crossroads. There was a walled mansion nearby. Desire for rest fought against the need to find her enemy. She staggered over to the roofed gateway. Thinking only to sit, she fell heavily against the door and was instantly asleep. Her staff slipped from her hand and banged against the Buddhist symbol on the door panels.

She was asleep when the small sally port by the gate opened and a broad heavy face looked out. Thoughtful eyes regarded her calmly for a moment. The thick lips pursed as they noted the crumpled girl. Okiku was barely conscious as black-clad brawny arms lifted her and carried her inside. She was laid on a ready pallet and stripped of her clothes. There was a whispered consultation of female voices, and then she was covered by a thick quilt. Exhausted sleep claimed her.

She woke to the hollow sound of a massive bell, and knew she was in a temple. The sight of black-clad female figures passing by told her she was in a nunnery.

The paper-covered shoji door slid aside with a whisper and a bald head peeked inside. Seeing Okiku was awake, the nun rose from her knees and glided silently to the pallet side where she knelt again. She placed her hand on Okiku's forehead.

'You seem to have recovered, my child. I will call for food.' She called out softly, and there was a quiet scurry of feet on the boards of the external corridor. Okiku tried to rise, but the nun firmly held her down.

'Not yet, my child. You are still weak, and we will take care of you.'

Okiku gratefully slumped back onto the pallet. Her stomach was rumbling with hunger, and she was well content to play the weakling for the meanwhile. The shoji slid aside again, and two young women entered bearing black lacquer trays. They arranged them in the middle of the room, not far from Okiku's side. Both bowed.

'Will that be all, lady?' one of them asked.

The prioress dismissed them silently, and they bowed and withdrew, closing the door behind them. Okiku noticed that both were quite beautiful, with clear pale skins, high cheekbones, and small rosebud mouths, though their shaven heads gave them an unusual appearance. She also noticed, and puzzled about, the sly glances both cast in her direction from their lowered heads.

The prioress motioned her to eat, and she seated herself diffidently on the seating cushion. Each tray held a large covered bowl of rice, a red lacquered bowl of soup, a dish of elaborate pickles cut in flower shapes, and a vegetable stew of radish, seaweed, and rice cakes. Murmuring polite acceptance, Okiku took her chopsticks and commenced to eat. They ate in silence. The prioress' sharp eyes took in every detail of Okiku's bearing, wandering from her face to her breasts, the tops of which were visible through her loose robe.

Both stew and pickles had been lightly flavoured with sake, and Okiku felt a warm lassitude spread through her body as she finished her meal. At last the prioress called out again, and the same two young nuns cleared away the remains. They surveyed Okiku again in much the same manner the prioress had.

'I am the prioress Gohei,' said the older woman. 'We are pleased to be able to assist you in your trouble at Dosojin-ji. We are a very small monastery – five nuns and myself – but I am sure we are well able to cater to your needs. Perhaps you would care to tell me your trouble, as I can see you are distraught.'

Okiku told her of the events at the ford, and the prioress nodded her sympathy.

'You are a young girl, and a virtuous one, since you accompany a nun on her pilgirimage. What of your family, however?' Again, Okiku resorted to telling part of the truth.

'My family are all dead, with the exception of

one uncle who lives in Ehime province. But I am under the protection of lord Miura,' she added cautiously.

The prioress smiled and moved to her side.

'I understand completely, my dear. The tragedy of the loss of your travelling companions is a terrible shock. You must overcome it. See how tense you are.' The prioress gently touched Okiku's arm and felt the muscles and tendons. She rocked her body and moved to kneel behind Okiku, testing the tenseness of the girl's shoulder and neck muscles.

'You need to learn to relax, girl. We at the Dosojin-ji temple must learn each in our own way to accept and ignore the World of Woe out there, but at least we can help you learn.' She gently probed the muscles of Okiku's shoulder, releasing the pent-up tiredness of her body. Okiku sat very still as the prioress' fingers explored her shoulders and then her back, and then dug into the sore spots in her body.

Okiku tensed again as her trained ears noted that someone, a very heavy someone, had seated himself outside the shoji door.

The prioress Gohei noted her alertness at once.

'Do not worry,' she breathed into Okiku's ear. 'It is merely Orin, our gatekeeper. She will maintain our privacy while I teach you the first of your lessons. She found you outside our door. She is a sumo wrestler from Shikoku Island: the only place where wrestling is practised by women. She is all the protection we need in these times.'

Okiku relaxed again as the warm breath tickled her ear and teased the sensitive nape of her neck. The prioress' knowledgeable fingers released the tensions in her body, and soon she noted, as the fingers dug lower into her back, that the older woman's warm breath was accompanied by almost ghostly touches of warm lips and tongue on her nape.

She wanted to turn around but the pleasure of the sensation hypnotised her into motionlessness. She felt the prioress release her loosely tied sash, and could hear her faint repetition of a Buddhist chant.

'Come, you must lie on your back so I can work on your relaxation properly.'

Without a will of her own, Okiku rose to return to the pallet, and her robe fell open. The prioress rose with her, and gently loosed the robe and let it drop to the floor. She admired the clean warm lines of the slim muscular body before her. Okiku was well muscled and bore herself proudly. The heart-shaped forest of hair at the juncture of her legs emphasised the flatness of her stomach and the erect curve of her black-tipped breasts.

The prioress led her to the pallet. She knelt before the passive girl and gently pressed the arches of her feet, and then the muscles of her calves. At each touch Okiku felt tension and resistance flow from the limb. She almost fell, and the prioress eased her to her knees. The finger touches continued, and Okiku felt her thighs become jelly and quiver at the weight of her body. The prioress bent forward and gently touched Okiku's chest between her breasts with her tongue. Again, the touch was almost imperceptible. Nonetheless, this time it sent messages of delight coursing down the girl's nude body. As her hands probed up Okiku's

102

thighs, releasing their muscles, the prioress' tongue moved up the cone of Okiku's right breast. At long last she reached the nipple and flicked it gently with her tongue. Shivers ran down Okiku's back. She would have pushed her entire body forward to feel more of the marvelous sensation, but for the fact that muscular control seemed to have been taken from her.

Gohei repeated the exercise on Okiku's left breast. Gently then, she pushed the unresisting girl over on her back. She sat erect on her knees for a moment, savouring the beauty of the sight. She slid her hands between Okiku's legs, and the girl languorously spread them. She watched the prioress' mouth, expecting the older woman to kneel forward and touch her cunt with one of those beautiful butterfly kisses. Instead, the prioress kept her eyes firmly on Okiku's and delicately probed the muscles of the girl's inner thigh.

Her fingers reached Okiku's pussy lips. With great care, she probed the outer lips of the girl's cunt. She found nerve endings that connected directly to her patient's brain. Sensations flashed upward from Okiku's pussy. The first touch brought a burning, raging lust. At a touch on another area of the lips, the burning sensation was replaced by a cool pleasure, like the one after an orgasm. Other touches brought other feelings as the knowledgeable prioress pushed and probed Okiku's folds.

With the thinking part of her mind Okiku noticed that though she was experiencing sensations that would normally have made her react physically, in this case her body did not respond at all to her lust. She wondered, in a detached way, what was happening to her. She had always been an active lover, promoting and guiding her own pleasure. This woman had made of her a passive doll.

The prioress' probing went on for what seemed forever to Okiku. She rose towards her climax several times. Each time her orgasm came, it seemed as if it were but a shadow of the real thing. Dimly she could glimpse another hill to be climbed, a better sensation. The prioress watched her coolly as she climaxed. Okiku's skin twitched, but otherwise one could not tell the storms that racked her body though by now she was shivering uncontrollably.

'My child, you are feeling the shadow of joy. Merely the shadow. This is the feeling of maya, of illusion. This is what our lord Amida meant by 'Yo': The world of illusion. Now you must be given to understand the taste of the Western Paradise.

She rose gracefully to her feet and stripped off her black gauze outer dress and the white robe she wore underneath. Her body was heavy but still pleasantly rounded. Small flat breasts had lost much of the firmness of youth, but her belly was firm and her thighs smooth and unwrinkled. To her surprise, Okiku noted that the prioress had shaved her body completely.

Swiftly, the older woman laid herself on Okiku. She fitted her legs on Okiku's and the girl felt their cunts touch and the folds intermesh. The sensation brought tears to her eyes. It was more delicate and enfolding than the feel of a man's prick, and while it lacked the satisfying feeling of male organ, it

104

touched every necessary part of Okiku's bottom lips and clit.

With great care, the prioress started shifting her weight on Okiku. She rolled and arched her body lightly. First she pressed down with two erect nipples onto Okiku's firm breasts. She moved her torso lightly from side to side, teasing the dark brown eruptions of flesh. Arching her back she then rocked back so that the tits were barely touching. Now the cunt folds meshed again. The prioress' somewhat bony mound pressed heavily against Okiku's clitoris which seemed to beg for more of the constriction. At the same time her trained sopping lower lips meshed with Okiku's. She shifted her weight slightly and Okiku felt the cuntal folds slither silkily over her own. She shuddered slightly, and the prioress Gohei increased the pressure on Okiku's lower parts.

All this time Gohei kept her eyes fixed firmly on Okiku's. Her face was calm and serene. She rocked on for a few minutes. Okiku started to move, attempted to stroke the firm back with her hand.

'No girl, you must learn to relax. This is the feel of the entrance to paradise.'

Now Gohei set to work to fuck Okiku in earnest. She wanted this fresh muscular girl to forget about men. She rubbed their cunts feverishly together. Her mouth murmured endearments and sucked Okiku's tits and mouth alternately. She probed Okiku's mouth with her tongue, and then with delicate fingers. The rhythm of their movements grew, and Okiku's breathing speeded up. At last the prioress stretched out on her with a sigh. Her body quivered and shook with the release of tension. Okiku shivered with pleasure. She clasped the prioress with her legs. Her rump pushed her up to an arch that joined the two mounds to one.

The nunnery was a small one. Okiku joined the nuns for their prayers. She was given the robes of a novice, but being the current pet of the prioress, was not made to share in all the work. At night she fell asleep exhausted nonetheless. She had had a hard time, and her body was not recovered.

She stayed in the nunnery for several days. The nuns, she saw, completed their prayers and religious duties conscientiously, but they did not deprive themselves of the pleasures of the body.

During the second night of her stay, she awoke to the sound of muffled giggling. Two warm bodies slipped into the covers with her. The two pretty young novices diddled her cunt for awhile. Growing bolder at her passivity, One of them mounted Okiku's spread legs. Something hard and familiar was shoved up her demanding cunt. She shivered and reached out. It was a harigata, a mock cock made of ivory in a V shape. One end was shoved into the novice's quim, the other probed Okiku. It was pleasant and unusual. The pressure of the girl's tits against her own, combined with the tireless thrust of the harigata, soon made Okiku's juices run freely.

She cried out loudly when the harigata brought her to a climax. The other girl ceased her movement after a frenzied shaking. She took the dildo out. It now felt like what it was – an inanimate piece of ivory. She liked to feel a cock shrivel and grow tiny inside her. She missed the feel of come gradually dribbling down her legs as a man withdrew. No, she decided, whatever a dildo's virtues, she preferred a man.

Okiku packed her belongings without haste. She was grateful to the nuns of Dosojin-ji temple but their way was not hers. True, she had learned from them and profited by their instruction, but her vengeance would not wait. She debated leaving the novice's robe she had been given. On the one hand, she did not want to abuse the temple's hospitality; on the other, she had been told it was a gift. She soothed her conscience by the well-worn expedient of promising to return it 'as soon as I am able.' She walked to the rear of the temple. The prioress had grown to like her. Their nightly love and instruction sessions had been pleasant, and she did not want to argue her right to exit with the massive gatekeeper or an enraged prioress. A quick leap brought her to the top of the cookhouse. Without pause she sprang to the tile-topped wall, and from there to the ground. She landed with bent knees and flexed hips in the fall known as 'butterfly on a flower'. She crouched motionless, waiting for an outcry. When there was none, only the frogs' protesting silence, which was soon broken by their renewed conversation, she set off on her way.

Hachiro, she knew, had been heading west towards Nagoya and Miyako. She could not leave the area, however, without a final prayer for the souls of her lovers and companions, drowned in the raging Tenryu river. She hurriedly walked the miles to the bank of the river, her mood becoming more sombre the closer she came to the scene of the tragedy.

The dark oppressed her as it had never done before. She had always loved the dark, had been taught its uses and pleasures. From childhood she had been trained in its delights, in preparation for the revenge to come. Now she felt alone. She had found her enemy, only to have him slip through her clutches in the dark.

Later that night she reached the river. It was a lonely stretch of the bank. There was a small river-porter's hut which she avoided, not caring for the company of her fellow man. She stood on the bank of the evil Tenryu river, cursing its kami. She had found the lover she had dreamed of all her life, and the river had stolen him away, as it had stolen the rest of her friends. And the dark had stopped her from finding them again, forever. Rubbing her hands together she repeated the formula taught her by the denizens of Dosojin-ji. 'We will meet again in Amida's Western Paradise.'

She turned her back on the river. She would follow her enemy again, since only vengeance was left. She climbed up from the bank and passed the porter's shack, half hidden by river reeds. A burst of laughter came from within. She sniffed. The porters had little to do with their miserable lives but gambling and the occasional cheap woman. She straightened her shoulders and started to march on her way. From the shack came a man's panicked scream. Okiku, unconcerned, walked on. She had taken only several steps when she heard another scream. She stiffened. The voice she had heard was familiar, coming from a dream. The man screamed again, and Okiku found herself creeping towards the shack.

She applied her eyes to a crack in the shack's mat-repaired walls and peered within. A group of loincloth-clad men were crouched around a candle that stood on a high candlestick. Over their intent heads she could see a pair of white legs clenched around a struggling stringy male butt. The woman called out again, a happy sound that Okiku had heard before. Without thought, she found her sword in her hand. As the man lying on Okiku arched his back and raised his head high, she cut through the wall of the shack with one silent slash. She marked her targets for a briefest moment and then acted. She threw the star-shaped steel *shaken* with care, and the candle flame died. In one step she had reached the circle of men. She transferred her sword from her left to her right hand, blade pointing forward from the fist in what was for her an unnatural position. The straight blade bit through the stringy neck and the screaming man ceased to be. She reversed her sword to its natural position, blade back from her fist, and the man closest to Rosamund, who was crouched over her ass, died. Mercilessly she hunted down the others. Untrained or not knowing, they cried out to one another, wanting to know what had happened, or fearing the worst, some sensing their doom cried 'No, no.' They made short work for a trained woman of Kaga.

She relit the candle. Rosamund was lying on her back, with her hands tied outstretched to a pole. A framework beneath her must have held her ankles, though they were loose now. In panic, Okiku saw that she was covered with blood. She rushed to her friend's side, but the gore had covered the blonde girl's torso so the Okiku could not tell if she was alive or dead. Her eyes fell on a small barrel of sake. She smashed it open and dashed its contents onto Rosamund's face. Some of the blood washed away. Rosamund's eyelids fluttered as she tried to peer out at the flood while still appearing to be dead. She caught sight of Okiku just as the latter dashed another measure of the pungent liquid at her face.

'Enough! You'll drown me. Stop, Okiku!' spluttered the blonde girl.

Okiku dropped the barrel and fell on Rosamund's prone body. She felt her body over and could find no wounds. She laughed and sobbed at the same time repeating endlessly, 'You're alive, you're alive.'

'Okiku! Okiku!' Rosamund tried to break into her friend's almost trancelike repetition. 'Let me loose, Okiku!'

The words finally penetrated to the dark girl's consciousness. Her eyes still streaming tears, she cut the bonds that ties Rosamund to the frame. Rosamund stretched and cried in pain. She had been tied for days, and tied in the same position for hours. Okiku gently assisted her to sit up.

'How did you get here?' they both asked simultaneously. They laughed at the similar thoughts.

'I've been here all the time. Since . . . since it happened, since the flood.'

'Like this?'

Rosamund nodded, then smiled impishly. 'It wasn't too bad. I enjoyed parts, except being tied all the time. They weren't as good as, as you . . . or . . .' She suddenly remembered the flood again,

110

and broke into tears, recalling those who had been snatched from her by the river.

Okiku shook her head in determination. 'No. I have found you again, against all odds. I found something else too, that I had been looking for for a long time.' She did not elaborate but her jaw clenched and Rosamund forbore to inquire. 'I shall find our men as well.' She stroked the beautiful plump breasts pressed against her shoulder.

Comforted, Rosamund sighed. 'I'm so tired, I must get some sleep. And decent food.'

Okiku nodded in agreement. 'But not here.'

'No,' shuddered Rosamund and looked around her.

'You must bathe,' Okiku urged her.

She stumbled to the river and rinsed the blood off her skin. When she returned she found that Okiku had eliminated all traces of their presence. The frame had been disassembled, her clothes removed, the ground cleaned of every trace of her lengthy stay.

'Won't they search for the killer of these men?'

'No,' said Okiku. 'These scum quarrel often among themselves and there are frequent murders among them. No one cares about them.' Her eyes were drawn to Rosamund's inner thigh.

'What is that?' she asked. The pinpricks were still bleeding. Rosamund sniffled. She was more concerned with the marring of her skin than with the minor pain.

'They marked me,' she said. 'They were going to sell me, and so wanted a permanent mark.' Her voice shook, and Okiku kissed her.

'It's only a tattoo, and we can only hope it's a

111

pretty one.' And there's nothing you can do about it anyway, my love, she thought to herself. Behind them, bodies began rotting in the rising heat of the day.

CHAPTER 10

By morning, the two women were far away from the Tenryu ford where bodies began rotting in the warmth of the day. They found the highway again. Rosamund had resumed her disguise, dressing in the outfit Okiku had received from the nuns, while Okiku resumed her pilgrim dress. They started the weary procedure of tracing the movements of their men.

It was three days before they found a clue.

'Yes,' said the owner of a tea shop where they stopped to drink. 'There was a sick samurai carried past in a litter one week ago or so. Largish man too, which is why I remember him.' He refilled their cups and offered another bean cake. 'Carried by lord Matsudaira's men I believe.' He lowered his voice. 'The scarfaced young one enfeoffed in Yoshida. I am glad I'm not in his fief, I'm ready to tell you. A hard master. Very hard indeed.' He shook his head and his topknot danced over his shaven pate. 'And you two ladies are travelling alone? Well, the country is peaceful now. Five, ten years ago, when the Osaka trouble was at its height, you would not have been able to do so safely. Why I remember . . .'

They rid themselves eventually of the garrulous teaman, and marched on.

'To Yoshida then . . .' said Rosamund. Her command of Japanese had increased by necessity, though Okiku still had to make excuses for her lack of speech by citing a vow of silence and meditation.

The following day the highway took them near the precincts of an ancient temple. Partly in search of information, partly out of a desire to rest, they entered the temple grounds. Hidden by a magnificent grove of cryptomeria, Honkoji temple instilled an atmosphere of deep peace and contentment, though the grounds yet showed little of the splendour that the gardens designed by Enshu would give it in the future. Scattered about were a multitude of small shrine structures and sacred objects. A huge oak was sanctified by the twisted straw rope that circled its bole. Some of the shrines were real miniatures, scarcely larger than a money chest. Others were large enough to contain complete meditation halls. Over them soared the many-angled roofs of the main temple.

They walked under a long row of square red-painted arches called torii, and came upon a smallish shrine flanked by two fox images. A young woman was repeatedly bowing before the shrine, sighing occasionally. They approached and she caught sight of Rosamund's nun's habit. She observed them for a while out of the corner of her eye as Rosamund and Okiku bowed and rubbed their hands in respect.

They straightened up, preparing to leave, when the young woman turned to them and bowed deeply. Okiku interposed her body between Rosamund and the stranger.

'Forgive me,' the young woman said. 'I am disturbing your devotions. If I may, may I request that the nun pray for my soul after I die?'

Okiku looked at her carefully. She was simply dressed, but the gown she wore was of expensive silk, and her kanzashi – long ornamented hairpins – were of fine silver workmanship. Her hairdo was a complex and expensive one and denoted a woman of the wealthy classes. Her face was slightly pockmarked, the pocks covered up by well-applied powder. When she bowed to them, Okiku was struck by the luminous quality of the skin at the back of her neck. Her dark eyes ready to fill with tears. Okiku wondered what such a woman was doing unescorted out of the mansion she obviously belonged in.

Okiku bowed in return and said, 'The nun will pray for you after death. Excuse me, but . . . have you no children to perform the office?'

The woman's eyes filled with tears again.

'No. Forgive me. Forgive me . . .' she repeated almost as an incantation. She squatted on the ground at their feet.

Okiku, who had troubles of her own and a tough nature, would as soon have ignored the woman as not. But Rosamund, struck by her piteous crying, knelt down beside her. Okiku perforce followed suit.

'Is there anything we can do to help you?' Okiku asked.

The woman rocked back and forth. 'I want to die,' she said eventually. 'I am useless to my lord

115

and to myself, and I want to die. I have not even served to delight the giant samurai enough to make him stay . . .' she wept silently.

'The giant samurai?' Okiku grasped her roughly by the lapels of her robe. 'What giant samurai? Tell me!'

The woman rocked on and shook her head 'No. It is too shameful a story. I cannot tell. All I wish is to die and be prayed for when I am in the land of Susuno-wo.'

Okiku shook her again impatiently. Rosamund pushed her aside hastily. 'Please tell us,' she said in a low voice as she tried to disguise her accent. 'He is a friend. We are looking for him . . .'

Okiku recollected herself. She knew she could get nothing out of the woman by force. Samurai woman would die first.

'Forgive me,' she said. 'I am concerned about the fate of . . . of my lover. He is a large man, a samurai from Miura. We were separated during the earthquake.'

The young woman looked at Rosamund and Okiku with her luminous eyes. 'I understand, I understand,' she whispered. 'He believed his friends lost . . . . That was the cause for his grief. My lord found no pleasure in him or me . . .'

'Do you know where he is?'

The young woman shook her head. 'I knew where he was several days ago – at the mansion of my lord Matsudaira in Yoshida. But he has since left . . .'

Okiku firmly raised her and led them to a comfortable seat on the porch of a nearby small shrine housing an image of Saint Jizo.

116

'Please tell us everything,' Okiku demanded. 'We must find him. Was there another man, a doctor, with him? And who are you?'

'My name is Oshin. I am a concubine of lord Matsudaira of Yoshida. Lord Matsudaira is fond of visiting the women's house, and also fond of . . .' she stuttered for a moment searching for the word '. . . diversion. He returned several days ago from a visit to the retired Shogun at the Castle in the Clouds at Sumpu, where he was commanded to appear.'

Okiku nodded. Old Ieyasu, the retired Shogun, still kept pulling the strings of government, though his grandsons were already grown men and his son had received the scroll of confirmation from the All Under Heaven, titular ruler of Japan. It was also known that Ieyasu, notwithstanding his age, was most interested in 'diversions' of sundry sorts.

'My lord felt the earthquake just after having crossed the Tenryu river. Some of the men in the vanguard of his train who were still on the bank found a bleeding young man washed ashore. Since he was a samurai, they reported it to my lord's bailiff. My lord Matsudaira then had him carried to his mansion. I was appointed to care for him. He was very big and strong and recovered quickly . . .'

. . . The swaying of the palanquin he rode on made Jiro nauseous. He tried to sit up, but waves of pain lashed him from his head downwards. He felt clumsily for his swords. The long one was nowhere to be found. The short one was reposing comfortably, as it should, near his head. He groaned in relief. A samurai without his wakizashi

117

– the shorter of his two blades – would be a laughing stock. His father, he knew, laughed at these 'murdering heathen customs' but he too was careful to carry both his swords, or at least the short one, in public.

A face appeared beside him. Squinting through the haze of pain Jiro could make out the headdress of a doctor. He sighed in relief.

'Goemon, are the girls well?'

A stranger's voice answered him. 'Don't try to speak. You are sick and wounded.' An evil tasting liquid was forced between his teeth and he lost consciousness.

When he awoke at last it was to the sound of soft high voices whispering and laughing around him. In the distance he could hear the twanging tones of an expertly played lute. In a room not far from him, a scar-faced young man, elaborately dressed, ignored the tableau before him and contemplated Jiro's fate with a crooked dreamy smile.

Jiro's head throbbed when he tried to sit up. A soft hand supported him. He turned, hoping for Okiku or Rosamund. A young woman, unknown to him and with peculiarly luminous eyes, was supporting him. She bent her head at his glance.

'I am Oshin. Please do not try to rise. You must still feel sick, and you have not eaten for a day. I will call for food.'

The food when it arrived was set in exquisite plates. For the first time in his life, Jiro tasted delicacies such as hatahata fish from Ugo and fresh picked tea. His strength returned with the food, which was served on trays near his pallet. Oshin helped him eat and regarded his appetite with what seemed like awe. Satisfied, he demanded his clothes.

'I am sorry. Clothes will be brought in a while. Your own have been lost.'

Two young girls, their flowing hair gathered at the nape with a bow, brought him a suit of clothes. There was a snow white, silken loincloth, a silk under-kimono, a grey shot silk over-robe, and a black striped silk sash. He stood to put on the cotton bathrobe Oshin held out to him. Behind a screen, thoughtful eyes roved over his form. The scarfaced young man smiled hungrily as the tall young man left the room.

The bath was as luxurious as the rest of the mansion's fittings. One side was open, and a small forest of dwarf bamboo in blue glazed pots invaded the bath and gave the atmosphere of bathing in a forest glen. It reminded Jiro of the circumstances of his meeting with Goemon, and his cock stiffened slightly at the thought.

The two young girls who had brought his meal stripped him of his robe. One of them gasped at the sight of his back. He had felt the pain before, but had ignored it. The doctor had treated the blow to his head, but the branch that struck him had tumbled him over the gravel of the river bed. He had saved himself by reflex action, curling into a ball, but his back and ass were covered with scrapes and abraded areas.

The two girls, under Oshin's supervision, gently bathed his back. Clean at last, he eased himself into the steaming water and allowed himself the luxury of a soak. Oshin knelt on a seat at the corner of the room. The two young girls, twins by their looks, knelt near the bath. Jiro could see their immature young nipples, as they had divested themselves of their outer robes. They smiled at his look, and one of them rose to add a stick to the fire that heated his bath.

Bath over, he was led back to his room. The corridors were deserted. Soft ladylike snores from behind some of the sliding doors told Jiro he was in the women's wing of the mansion. He wondered about that. Daimyo lords did not commonly allow low-ranking samurai lodging in their women's quarters.

The room was set for sleeping. The pallet was remade on the floor, and several candles lit the scene. The sliding doors were painted with gilt-scenes representing pheasants in courting plumage. Jiro felt uneasy in the room. The two young girls stripped of his cotton robe and folded it beside his waiting new robes. As they untied his sash and loosened the bathrobe, each of the young girls contrived to touch his quiescent prick. He struggled to hold his pose. Oshin, on her knees near the pallet as she directed operations, ignored the stirring of his member. One of the girls folded down the top coverlet. It was a warm night, and the coverlet was merely a light quilt without padding. He lay down, wondering if they would leave or join him. His prick gave another stir and began to stiffen. Pretending to help him into bed solicitously, the two girls made sure to feel his cock again. It stood out from his body. Oshin did not react visibly, though her eyes were directed intently at the sight. With a final flicker of their soft fingers and a giggle behind their hands, the two young girls left.

Jiro lay on his side in bed, watching Oshin and wondering whether she intended staying there the whole night. Instead, she rose to her feet and then knelt at the pallet side.

'Are you very sore?' she asked in a colourless tone.

'Not too much. Merely uncomfortable.'

'Surely a samurai should not mind some minor pain?' she asked suddenly. Her face, he noted, was lightly pocked, but her mouth was wide and pleasant looking. She had not stained her teeth black, a fashion that was catching on among upper class women, but which he, with his rural background found odd.

'No,' he answered her question. 'I am merely a bit stiff . . .' He wondered if the imposing mansion had made his tongue stiff as well. He tended to speak much more formally than usual, he noticed.

'Please lie on your back.'

He stared at her for a moment. She repeated her request, touching him lightly on the hip.

He grunted slightly as he lay back, his head on a high pillow which kept his newly set and oiled topknot away from the sheet.

Without any visible change of expression, she stripped the cover from him and laid her hand on his prick. It gave a single throb and stood out the length of his belly. She stroked it gently with her hand. It was dry and throbbing, and her smooth hand cooled his skin. She bent forward and ran her tongue from tip to balls. His prick glistened as it became covered with saliva. She rubbed the length of it again. She tried to keep her expression neutral, but there was a slight gleam of satisfaction and interest at the length and breadth of the erect rod. She stroked it again, then raised the tip and held the stiff length of meat perpendicular to Jiro's muscular belly. It looked as if she was shaking hands with another arm. She let the cock drop and it fell back tensely and slapped his muscular belly. Jiro laughed silently. She then raised his ball bag. Rather than letting it flop – Jiro tensed at the thought – she let it down gently between his legs.

He reached out and touched her breast through the thick fabric of her robe. She ignored his probing hands and continued playing with his prick. Again she raised it vertically, and then began a milking motion with both soft palms. He pulled at her robe and the under-robes beneath until he could slip them off and bare her body. Since kimonos are untied except by the sash, this was easily accomplished without disturbing her own activities.

She had firm full breasts that swayed from side to side with the movement of her hands as she vigorously masturbated him. He pinched her rather flat nipple with finger and thumb, and the fleshy bud rose under him. He squeezed the breast harder, but when he attempted to pull him to her, she wriggled her shoulders without ceasing the motions of her hands and his hands fell away from her body.

He tried again, and again she evaded him. All the time she concentrated on the huge prick before her, sucking it gently and firmly. Her eyes never left Jiro's crotch, and her lips pursed in concentration.

A tiny drop of clear fluid appeared at the tip of his prick. With a birdlike movement she bent forward and quickly sipped it up. Her full breasts

122

hung tantalizingly for a moment. He allowed their full soft weights to push against the back of his hand. Again, she gave no conscious sign that she noticed what he was doing to her body.

He flipped aside the skirt of her robe and slipped his hand into the opening to touch her thigh. It was warm and full. He felt her from the knee up, through the folds of robe layers and petticoat until his probing fingers found a trace of rough hair.

His fingers squirmed and scratched through her patch, looking for the spot that would make her react. She still dealt with his prick impassively, now and again bending forward to capture a drop of fluid. At last he found her slit. He tickled the lips softly at first, and when that brought no response, pushed harder. Finally goaded, he shoved aside her robe and forced his whole palm between her legs.

In contrast to her cool expression, he found her cunt burning like a furnace. The inside surface of her thighs was damp. He pushed questing fingers deeper between rather thin lips and fingered the length of her cunt as Okiku had taught him. His fingers slid lubriciously through the overflowing moisture.

He tried to raise himself slightly and spread her thighs, but suddenly she was gone. With one motion she rose gracefully to her white-socked feet and slid the gown back over her shoulders. She gave him one long sphinxlike look, bowed to him, and drew back. Before she blew out the candle that illuminated the room, he saw that her gaze had flicked to the screen at the other side of the room. The sliding door sighed twice, and she was gone.

As she stepped out, Jiro thought he heard a

123

second sound echoing the sliding door. He lay back on his pallet, frustrated. His erection throbbed and he stroked it savagely for awhile, thinking viciously of what he would do to the minx when she came to his bed again. Then a thought struck him. He rose quietly in the dark, unsheathed his wakizashi, and stole carefully across the golden soft tatami mats to the gold lacquered screen at the other end of the room. Behind the screen was another sliding door, and a single rich sitting pad. He felt the pad. It was still warm. Puzzled but still hopeful he returned to his bedding. He fell asleep still expecting to be awakened by a soft, curious hand. Before he drifted off he heard a burst of ragged laughter hidden by the labyrinthine corridors of the mansion.

Jiro woke still wearing an enormous hard-on. It had barely subsided by the time Oshin and the two girls returned. After breakfast and a bath they dressed him in the fancy silk clothes and white socks that had been provided the evening before. The young serving girls giggled at his semi-erect cock and contrived to touch it as often as possible. Oshin wore as inscrutable an expression as before. Again they refused to answer questions as to his immediate future. The girls merely giggled. Oshin apologised profusely.

'Our lord will explain if he wishes when he sees you,' was all she was prepared to venture.

His cock rose to its full length under their ministrations, and unfurled like a massive branch while they dressed him. Without any embarrassment one of the girls tucked it into his loincloth, winding the belly wrappings about so as to smooth the line of his robe.

They conveyed him through a series of corridors with polished wood floors. The sliding doors they passed were all closed, though Jiro could hear the sounds of life inside them: movements, quiet feminine conversations, the smell of tobacco. They passed several indoor courtyard gardens, all exquisitely laid out. The chrysanthemums, Jiro noted, were in full bloom.

After a last bend in the corridor, they stopped before a door. The two girls knelt and slid the double doors apart. They stepped into an anteroom and stopped, and the girls slid the doors shut. Oshin and Jiro were in a large, well-appointed waiting room. To one side was a niche with a small flower arrangement of silvery susuki grass, green berries on a branch and red blossoms. Before them was another double door guarded by two kneeling samurai, fully armed with short and long swords. They were dressed in wide-shouldered formal overcoats, and their hands rested unpleasantly near their sword hilts.

The two swivelled as one and still on their knees slid the double doors open. Oshin and Jiro knelt before the threshold.

'Excuse me. The young man is here,' she said in a loud musical voice.

'Come in.'

They rose and stepped through the doorway, and it slid shut behind them. Jiro knelt again and stayed motionless on his knees. Oshin walked quickly ahead and to the left and knelt facing the figure before them. Jiro studied the room and its occupant quickly.

The fittings and tatami mats were of the finest quality. The sliding doors to left and right were decorated with a riot of flowers in full bloom: a set depicting spring and autumn. Directly before him was a slightly raised dais surfaced with tatami mats. A young man in elaborate brocade robes, his topknot a ruler-straight line dividing his shaven forehead perfectly into two parts, was seated on a silk cushion. He was leaning his left elbow negligently on an armrest. Behind him rose a sword in antique fittings of gold and enamel.

Two things drew Jiro's attention immediately. The young lord's face was disfigured by two crossed scars that ran from chin to temples and crossed over his upper lip. His face was drawn into a perpetual snarl. With his right hand he was languidly busy. A young woman dressed in elaborate hairdo and white socks knelt on all fours before him. Her face was to Jiro, and he could see that the man on the dais was painting something on her ass in delicate strokes of his brush. She looked up, saw Jiro and blushed. She turned scarlet from her face to the tips of her dangling breasts.

The young man paused in his painting for a moment and stared at Jiro.

'What is your name?'

'I am Miura Jiro. My father is a retainer in the service of the Shogun.'

'I've heard of him,' grunted the other. 'The foreigner. What are you doing here?'

'I was on a pilgrimage to the shrines in the Kansai

126

area. I was separated from my companions by a flood. Your men rescued me.'

The young man looked at Jiro with flat black eyes. The girl before him twitched, and he slapped her rump, then resumed his painting. After several minutes of absorption in his task he spoke again.

'You will stay here for awhile. Eventually you may perhaps proceed on your journey.'

Jiro knew better than to argue. Oshin regarded him silently, most of her attention on the doings of her lord. The young lord at last spoke to her.

'He will stay for awhile.' Then he nodded with his head in obvious command. She rose and stepped over to where Jiro was seated on his knees.

'Stand up,' she whispered.

He stood, and without ceremony she loosened and removed his sash, and then removed his robes. At first dazed with the events, he was ready to protest when her whispered feverish 'Don't' penetrated his consciousness. He remembered where he was. There were men behind these sliding doors who would cut him to meat at the slightest order of the lord before him. He submitted quietly.

He stood there, a tall, brawny young man with a huge muscled chest. His hands, used to handling carpenter's tools as well as weapons and writing brush, were unusually large. His father had insisted that all his sons be shipwrights as well as samurai.

The young lord's jaw moved, whether in approval or disapproval, Jiro could not tell. He nodded again at Oshin, now kneeling at Jiro's feet. She swivelled slightly and stripped off his loincloth and the remains of his dignity. Unmoving outwardly, he was composing a suitable revenge on

127

this scarfaced tormentor. His prick swung placidly from the forest at the juncture of his legs.

The young man stared at Jiro's prick and balls for a long moment. So did the young woman before him. Again the lord motioned to Oshin. She took the flaccid member in her hand and milked it a couple of times. Jiro tried to control his reactions. The scarfaced man moved his jaw again. Oshin redoubled her efforts.

'Use your mouth for a little while,' her master commanded.

She opened her mouth and slid the soft cock over her lips and tongue. She was so expert at her task that Jiro could not feel her teeth at all. Warmth and moisture enclosed him. Involuntarily his prick began growing. She hollowed her cheeks and sucked powerfully at his prick. It unfurled in her mouth. She rolled the fleshy rod about with her tongue, and with each movement, exquisite thrills ran through Jiro's frame.

'Enough!'

Her mouth withdrew suddenly. Jiro's prick was at that half-erect stage where it stuck forward horizontally. Even so, it was an impressive sight. Its blind eye stared the painted girl full in the face, and she returned the look with interest. The lord pursed his scarred lips and nodded.

'Look at my painting,' he ordered Jiro. 'Go and kneel before him,' he told the girl.

She rose to her feet. She was short and plump, with small tits that barely juggled as she moved. Between her thighs Jiro could see faint pinker stripes on the pale skin. He wondered what they were. She tried to keep her face impassive, but shame and hopeful lust seemed to peer out alternately from her eyes.

She knelt before him and presented a full rounded ass for his inspection. It was covered by an elaborate, multi-coloured painting of the finest detail. Jiro's prick rose stiffer at the sight of the ass presented to his view. He became caught up in the excitement of the moment.

'Look closer!'

He knelt behind the girl and peered at the painting in wonder. The scene depicted a country picnic of men, women and demons in the maki-e style. Gold paint was lavishly used, and each figure of the twenty or so bore its own stamp of personality. Three demons were hurrying out of their home in the ground, the hole formed appropriately by her ass. A woodcutter peered out of the forest in which paint blended with straight black hair. The characters were whimsical and individualised. Jiro was no expert on paintings, though he had, by necessity, been taught to distinguish good brushwork from bad. The painting however appeared exquisite, and far better executed than many he had seen.

'Ah,' said the lord. 'I see you are impressed. My paintings will not survive me, you see. This is as it should be. This World of Woe will end; why should I leave anything to anyone else.' His eyes stared at nothing and he seemed to be talking to himself.

He directed his attention back to Jiro who was studying alternately the painting and the semi-gaping cunt exposed to his view.

'Oshin! Stick him into her.'

His concubine moved to obey.

129

'Lord!' protested Jiro, 'it will ruin the painting!'

'Do it!' The young lord ignored Jiro's protest, as if he had not spoken.

She took Jiro's erect tool in her hand and drew him, like a hypnotised rabbit to a snake, to the waiting cunt. 'Don't use your hands at all!' she whispered to him, almost unheard.

He shuffled forward obediently. Oshin moved the rampant purple tip of his prick about the girl's lower lips for a little while to start the juices flowing. The kneeling girl lowered her head to the floor, and her hairdo obscured her face from Jiro's view. Slowly, using her hand as a control, Oshin fed the giant cock into the girl's expectant cunt.

Jiro's cock was again engulfed in a warm, moist cavern. The girl was not too tight, but the folds of her cunt soothed his heated and rearing member. He wanted to thrust forward powerfully, but Oshin's contolling hand limited his movements. She drew his fleshy sword out of the other girl, and the painted one sighed. Oshin stabbed again, and then again, Jiro's staring eyes saw almost nothing. His body trembled at the effort.

His trance was broken when Oshin pulled his cock completely from the waiting cunt and brandished it in the air like a warrior giving a salute. The young lord stared at the stained weapon before his eyes. He licked his lips convulsively for a moment.

'Do what she's doing!' he ordered Oshin. Her face registered no emotion as she stripped of the multiple layers of her robes.

Jiro knelt paralysed. His body and his prick were both erect as he saw Oshin's full breasted body emerge palely from its brocade cocoon. She knelt beside the other girl, her eyes on her master. The lord raised his eyes from Jiro's prick and looked at his eyes.

'Put yourself first in one, then in the other,' he ordered.

Jiro leaned forward and eased himself into the fresh hole before him. He longed to squeeze the full breasts, but her whispered warning still rang in his ears. He shoved his cock the full length into her waiting cunt. The warm moist walls gripped his cock and parted reluctantly before his passage. He rested for a short moment, soaking in her juices. Then his body urged him to withdraw again.

He tried to thrust forward, but was frustrated by Oshin, who moved her ass and indicated the other one. He shifted his position awkwardly and guided his cock with his hand into the waiting orifice. The painting was now stained and smeared, and his hairs and balls held the evidence and sparkled with colour.

He alternated in this way for awhile. His breath came in gasps as he fought for control. The scar-faced lord, Jiro noticed, was following the action with growing interest. His eyes were glittering, and his tongue emerged more frequently to lick his lips. The scars on the man's lips glistened as he wet them, though his tongue seemed to touch the horny tissue with reluctance.

Jiro was unsurprised to see the young lord stand and drop his robes to the floor. He had a thick straight prick which bowed at every step he took. Jiro, though doubtful of the lord's intentions, continued his alternating thrusts. The painted girl was sighing quietly with every thrust. Soon, Jiro knew, she would reach her climax and he soon after. He only hoped Oshin would reach hers before him.

The young lord stood watching the three on the floor for awhile. The women were familiar to him, and he expected little from them. The young samurai, on the other hand, was all he could have hoped for.

'Stop!' he commanded. 'Oshin, roll over.'

Jiro stopped his thrusts. The painted girl whimpered faintly in frustration. Jiro clenched his fists. Oshin lay herself on her back, knees in the air. Her face, Jiro noted, was as composed as before, but sweat beaded her upper lip, and her eyelids were twitching. Signs of some changes within, he thought hopefully.

'Enter her!' commanded the other man.

Jiro lay himself flat with alacrity. He stretched out on Oshin. With one heaving thrust he was buried to the balls in her tight cunt. He felt his bag smack against her ass, and the juicy sound made him push into her with renewed frenzy. Oshin raised her legs and with surprising strength clasped his body to hers. Her arms went about his heaving shoulders and her long nails dug into his flesh. She locked her heels about him in an octopus embrace as they rocked together.

He was not surprised to notice that the scarfaced lord hurried over behind him. Like all of his time and place, he had in his youth had experience of other men. But he had always been the aggressor, the pleasure was limited, and he much preferred the other sex. Sex with men, he had long ago decided, was for boys.

The lord paused behind him, and Jiro tensed, expecting and hating the entry. Instead he heard a cry of rage. A sharp slap resounded in the room, and Oshin whimpered in pain.

'You fool,' her master cried. 'He's spoiled, spoiled do you hear?' Blows fell indiscriminately on Oshin's legs and thighs and Jiro's ass. 'He's full of scars and scrapes. How can I enjoy something worthless like this. Get off her, you fool.' He hit out roughly at Jiro's gravel-scarred ass and back.

The enraged baron raved at them as they disentangled themselves. Jiro saw that his eyes were staring and he practically frothed at the mouth. He panted heavily, and at last regained enough calm to return to the dais.

'Come here!' he motioned to the painted girl. She hesitantly approached. He pulled her down, ass to him. He rose slightly, still glaring at Oshin and Jiro, and thrust himself brutally into her. She gave a restrained cry, and then crouched passively.

'Get out, get out, Oshin,' he panted at them. 'Take this monster with you. Keep him. When he is recovered from his . . .' the words seemed to stick in his throat '. . . from his scars, bring him back for my use. I will decide what to do with him. Now GET OUT!' The last words came out in a scream, and the young lord pumped his cock viciously into the girl. She moaned slightly, but as they crept back out of the room, Jiro could see that she was beginning to respond to the treatment.

CHAPTER 11

Jiro spent the rest of the day in a room. He wanted to go out, to see the garden beyond the sliding doors. Oshin stayed with him and prevented him. He was still in the women's quarters of the mansion, and the lord did not care, he thought, for a strange buck among his does.

His temper wore thin as the day wore on. The two twin servant girls brought their meals as before. Oshin was sunk in gloom and would not talk. He tried meditating, and then exercise, but both activities merely made him think more acutely of Oshin, sitting positively still before the exit.

When nightfall came, and with it the laying of his pallet, he was beyond caring. The two girls left, after their usual antics while dressing him. Oshin still sat by the door. He could see himself reflected in her eyes. He sat on the bed in his cotton robe staring back at her. The sole candle illuminated the scene.

He took a deep breath and expelled it slowly. He was on his feet with one motion. Approaching her across the room he remembered the servant girl in his father's barn. There would be no repeat of THAT, he vowed grimly.

135

He towered over her for a moment. She gave no sign of noticing his presence. He quickly crouched by her side and ran his arms around her hips. He dug his hands under her folded shins and stood erect. She came up with him, a compact resisting bundle. He lowered her on the bed, still in her kneeling pose. There was a gleam of what he took for approval in her eyes. He stripped off her kimono rapidly, one hand ready to pin her if she objected. He pushed her back onto the soft pallet, and without any preparation, entered her.

She was as soft and as moist as before. He moved strongly into her. His large body covered hers, and she could feel the roughness of his chest hairs as they pressed against her tits. His climax was too sudden for her. He had been through much, and his prick was spurting its milky fluid before he was in any way ready. He wriggled his ass as he came, driving his pubis against hers, exciting her for more.

She waited passively to see what he would do. He lay on her breast breathing heavily, but not withdrawing. His cock was still as stiff as before. He started moving again. This time she moved with him. Her arms came over his back, and she clasped him to her with delight.

This time he felt the clipping sensation of her cunt as she came beneath him. He crushed her under him powerfully, squeezing out her breath. Still she came in soft jerks, moaning his name over and over.

They lay together later. His prick still soaked in her cunt. He traced his fingers lazily over the curves of her body. She happily allowed him everything

136

he cared to do. He explored her mouth with his tongue. His fingers poked into her holes and crannies.

Gradually his movements became more purposeful. She moved together with him, but besides holding his shoulders when he mounted and moved into her, she was a passive lover. He parted her legs widely and began moving in her velvety cunt again. She moaned protestingly when he rammed a questing digit into her puckered asshole, but quieted when he filled her mouth with his tongue.

Her climax was sudden and unexpected. Jiro was far from ready. Still holding himself in her, he rolled over onto his back. He made her squat on him, feet on the mat near his hips. Then he grasped her thin hips and raised her till the tip of his prick just barely kissed her hole. Gently he lowered her down so that their hairs met in a tangled sopping mass. He raised her again and lowered her, this time with greater force. He repeated the motion again and again, until her eyes glazed and her belly twitched with the power of her orgasm. He came at the same time, slamming her down onto his chest and arching his body into a bridge, the peak of which threatened to tear her body to pieces.

They lay on the pallet most of the following two days. Jiro was still not allowed to leave the room. The twin serving girls brought his food, made his bed, accompanied him to his bath, and dressed him morning and night. They giggled incessantly behind their hands while doing so, and played with his cock, which, as soon as they left the room, he employed on Oshin's willing body.

He fucked her often, and between times they

talked. He was the first one who had ever listened to her talk, and taken an interest in what she had to say. Gradually, over the following few days, between one fuck and the next, usually with his prick still in her sopping cunt, she told him her story.

She was the daughter of a low-class samurai, a retainer of her lord. The lord had heard of her beauty and had accepted her into his House of Women. Her father had, in due course of time, received a larger grant and raise in status.

She was content with this. As a woman of her class she had little will of her own, and no rights. Her lord was gentle and though he had several women, was generally kind and a good lover.

Then came the war. Lord Matsudaira had gone to join his clan and his liege lord, the Shogun, in the siege of Osaka. He had come back a scarred and changed man. A Toyotomi warrior had slashed his face twice before being killed by the daimyo's bodyguards. The bodyguards had committed seppuku, but the cuts had not healed for many months. During that time, the young lord had taken up several amusements. His entourage of women had grown, and young samurai were pressed into service as well. His entertainments had taken a gruesome turn, and some of his victims had died. Oshin looked at Jiro sadly as she said this, but he, engrossed in playing with her erect nipple, had paid no attention.

Oshin herself had remained as she was. She took no pleasure in the beatings her lord administered before mounting her, nor in the humiliations and

138

tricks she visited on others at his command. But she had been bred for loyalty, and loyally she served.

'Well, fucking is fucking, and you can at least enjoy that. Besides, he doesn't seem to be a jealous type,' said Jiro complacently.

'He only wanted you. He enjoys humiliating people so he had me and someone else present. Pain is his pleasure.'

'I know someone like that,' grinned Jiro. 'That she enjoys getting it, rather than giving.' His grin turned sombre as he realised that he would have to wait awhile before being able to join his friends.

'What do you know about it?' Oshin said. 'Didn't you see the lash marks on the girl he wanted you to fuck?'

Jiro kissed her placatingly. 'No. I wouldn't want him to mark you.'

The big baby seems unaware that Lord Matsudaira does not behave any different towards men than towards women, thought Oshin. And strangers had disappeared in the mansion before . . .

Oshin was careful not to talk when they heard the sliding door behind the gold washed screen move. Jiro, conscious that he was being watched and enjoying the feeling, took great care to perform well. At times like those, he thrust into Oshin unceasingly, and she moaned with a delight she had not found in sex before.

A futher indication of the lord's perverse nature arrived soon enough. Oshin and the serving girls entered the room on the noon of the third day of his incarceration. Her face bore no trace of emotion as she sat herself down formally on her knees near the closed door and bowed in his direction. The two serving girls arrayed themselves behind her.

'The lord has ordered a special task for you. These two,' she indicated the servant girls with her hand, 'are virgins, which he doesn't care for. You will deflower them in preparation for his pleasure.'

Jiro looked at the two girls in amazement. He noticed now that they were more heavily made up than usual. Their hair hung down to their waists, their lips were painted in brilliant scarlet. Both wore plain silk sleeping robes, with the ties of their sashes in front. His prick rose to attention as he saw that though they tried to remain impassive, there was an anticipatory gleam in their eyes.

'You must do it quickly, and not delay, as Lord Matsudaira is anxious to have them please him.'

Jiro's ears heard the delicate sliding sound of the door behind the gold screen as she spoke. He bowed to Oshin and smiled.

'I am ready to do all that is possible.'

The girls gave him enigmatic smiles, and spoke for the first time in his hearing.

'We are twins. You must do us together,' said one.

'Together?' he echoed. 'I've only one prick.' He opened the fold of his silk robe and extracted the article in question from its confines. His machine rose proudly, the purplish head as hard as a blunt arrow.

The two girls giggled. They hurried over to the pallet. One of them lay down, legs in the direction of the screen. The other loosened her sash and opened the robe, exposing her to view. Bemused, Jiro stood above them. The second girl stripped herself naked. She then laid herself flat on the first one, cunt to cunt, and tits kissing.

'Hurry, Get out of your clothes,' she ordered. The tone was so peremptory and out of character for a serving woman, that Jiro obeyed with a laugh. Both girls were thin and somewhat underdeveloped. The muscular buttocks of the one with her back to him twitched expectantly. The lower one moved some hair out of her eyes and looked at his erect cock while licking her lips.

'It's so big . . .' she murmured. The two kissed passionately.

'Now! First one of us, then the other. One strike each!'

The familiar fencing phrase used in this context made Jiro laugh again. He knelt behind the two girls, and using his hand probed gently for the opening. Both cunts were almost hairless, and the lips seemed to search out his pole.

'Fool! What kind of samurai are you?' berated one of them. 'Find the place at once and strike! Both of us, immediately. We want to lose it together!'

He drew back a bit and contemplated the two joined cunts before him. There was little to tell them apart. Both slits were clearly visible. They blended into one another giving the appearance of a long narrow single cunt, fringed lightly with hair. Like a swordsman preparing to strike, he held himself still for one moment, concentrating his energies and stilling his breathing. He leaned forward, and with a strong thrust of his belly and thigh muscles, ripped his way into the upper of the two cunts. He pushed forward with all his might,

141

while uttering a strong 'kiai' sound. There was momentary resistance, then the feel of his cock sliding up a narrow channel that constricted his movement. The girl let out a shriek, but lay still under him. He pushed further in until his hairs scratched the moons of her ass, and both girls were crushed under his weight.

The one in whose cunt he was lodged moaned as he probed her deepest recesses. She moaned again as he withdrew. He could see tears start in her eyes. The other one watched her sister with wide-eyed delight.

Without pause, Jiro aimed his weapon lower and drove his fleshy sword into the girl on the bottom. Again the slight resistance and the scream, and he was lodged securely in her. He shook his body lightly and started to move himself comfortably in her. The upper girl bucked and arched her body and the lower one clawed him backwards. Surprised, he let go and pulled his rampant cock out of her depths.

The two girls grinned at him through tear-stained faces. Naked as they were, they scampered behind the gilded screen at the far end of the room. They left a trial of blood spots behind them. Jiro heard the sliding door shut behind them and one other. Soon he could hear two girlish voices crying aloud in pleasure and pain from the neighbouring room. He stared at the screen in bewilderment and frustration. Oshin was suddenly standing over him as he squatted. She pushed her skirts aside, and without a word impaled herself on his bloodstained prick, and with a quick squeeze of her cunt brought him to a fountaining climax. She smiled at his dazed expression, and bit his massive chest.

'Many men have performed that particular office for him,' she said composedly. 'But this time I've had the benefit of it.'

He raised her and himself and carried them to the pallet to continue their pleasure. The sounds of wild and frenetic activity in the neighbouring room continued.

He fell asleep that night, happily exhausted. When he awoke, it was pitch dark. There was a sound of movement near his head. He opened his eyes slowly, wondering whether to search for his wakizashi, sheathed by his head, but it was only Oshin. She was fully dressed and sat on her knees by his head.

'What is it?' he asked sleepily.

'Lord Matsudaira has determined that you will soon be well enough to attend him,' she said in the colourless voice she maintained for such pronouncements.

'Well, good,' he grumbled. 'It's time he had what he wanted and I got out of here.'

She drew in a breath sharply, and then bent to whisper in his ear.

'No!! You must get out. Leave at once!'

He tried to pull her into bed with him, but she resisted passively. At last he desisted.

'Why?' he asked.

'The lord has had several young travellers brought here. Some did not want to come. All wanted to leave once they had arrived. None have left. You must go quickly, before he notes your absence.'

'Where are they, these travellers?' he chided gently. 'Life here is surely no worse than on the road?'

'Fool! They'll never leave! Don't you understand? If the reports of his kidnappings and practices reached shogunal ears, he would be removed! You are the first samurai he has brought here. Do you think he will let you go? He knows you are only a second son and no great search will be made for you. You must go at once.'

The urgency of her speech penetrated through his good nature and the haze of sleep. Jiro sat up, still naked.

'He can't do this!' he protested. Even to his own ears the protestation sounded thin. A daimyo baron was supreme in his own fief, particularly one of the Matsudaira family: relatives of the shogunal family. If by chance news of his murder by the mad daimyo reached other ears, his father might be allowed to declare a feud, but he was only a lower ranking hatamoto. The shogunal government MIGHT take action, but only if there were other circumstances that necessitated the removal of the baron.

He made up his mind in a flash, and hurriedly began dressing in the dark. She looped his sash around him as he stood and bent down to tie the skirts of his hakama split trousers. When she rose, she handed him a long heavy bundle. It was his long sword which she had stolen from the sword rack at the entrance to the mansion.

In silence she took him through the maze of corridors, interlocking rush-matted rooms, and the garden to the wall of the mansion. A convenient plum tree offered a way of passage, though he would have to jump on the other side.

'What about you?' he whispered.

She shook her head. 'I have my duty. I must stay. I am his.'

'But he'll kill you! You yourself say he is mad!'

She straightened her back proudly. 'Do you think this is the life I want? But I am the daughter of a samurai. I must do my duty by my lord.'

He tried again to persuade her to come with him. She urged him hurriedly off, then watched with tears in her eyes as he scaled the wall and dropped off the other side.

'. . . That is the last I saw of him. My lord did not dare to make open enquiries as to his present whereabouts, but he has set his police force and spies quietly to the task. I have heard no more about him,' Oshin concluded her tale. 'Now, I have only one wish, and that is to die.'

'You can come with us,' Rosamund proposed generously. 'We too are looking for him.' Okiku scowled at her.

'No.' Oshin said. 'I have begged my lord to allow me to die for failing to stop the young samurai's escape. I was responsible for him. He beat me for several days. Worse, he has forbidden me to commit suicide and has ejected me from his presence. I shall stay at this temple, near the site of my birth, until I am permitted to die.'

Rosamund looked at the young woman in bewilderment. Okiku, who understood the concept of duty, merely bowed to Oshin in pity, and tugged the blonde girl to her feet.

145

'We must go now. Please be released from this sorrow. We must continue looking for our friend. I am sorry that our joy is derived from your pain.'

They walked out of the shrine on the way to Yoshida, full of hope. Behind them, the first blush of the maple, and a rich kimono hid the sight of tears.

CHAPTER 12

For Jiro, the past weeks had been difficult. Trying to reach Osaka, the object of their journey, with the hope of finding his friends, was entangled with his need to avoid capture by lord Matsudaira's retainers. He was too big to be inconspicuous, and thus had to move away from the highway and the travel-control barriers. He gradually worked his way north, into the Kaga mountains. The days grew chill, and the nights cold. He existed partly on roots and mountain vegetables he came across, partly on rice he managed to buy from farmers he met. Once he found a crop of delicious matsutake mushrooms, which grow only in pine forests. He gorged himself on the smoky tasting flesh.

He paused high on a slope and looked down at the hamlet below him. There was one large house, probably belonging to a low-class samurai-farmer. The other houses were smaller, with the high pitched thatched roofs common to the area. It was late afternoon and thin trills of smoke rose in the air. Around him rose the huge forest-coated mountains of Kiso. Beyond them unclimbed peaks shone with snow.

He chewed his lips in thought. He had tried to

make his way to the plains to the west and south. An overhead remark had sent him fleeing deeper into the mountains. The two woodsmen he had overheard early in the morning had been told to look for a giant samurai, by whom or what they did not know. Now he had to decide whether to try the village for food.

He looked down at his clothes. They were torn and filthy. His pate had not been shaven for a week. His hair hung like rat tails. He looked, he thought wryly, precisely like a mountain robber.

Hunger was the deciding factor. He slid down the slope as quietly as he could. He would try, he decided, one of the poorer houses. At one end of the hamlet he noted a small house. The wooden boards were warped. Green moss grew on the thatch and it sagged in places. Stones kept the material down. From the hut came the welcome smell of cooking rice, and a light beckoned through the slits between the boards.

He straightened his shoulders and swaggered a bit as he approached. Trying to ingratiate himself would do no good. Commoners expected samurai to be arrogant, even poor ones, and to act otherwise would raise their suspicions. Perhaps the residents of the house would be so relieved at his politeness, he mused, that they would share their meal with him. He slid open the small door, bowed and cried out, 'Excuse me for disturbing you . . .' his loud cry trailed off.

He had expected a hovel, but the largish room he found himself in was pleasantly appointed. Clean mats covered the raised wooden floor. There were some agricultural implements hung on the walls of the packed earth entrance area. The men lolling on the raised floor of the room were not, however, farmers. Jiro cursed himself silently. The smell of cooking rice should have alerted him. Such a poor house could not afford to cook rice twice in a year. The men stared at him coldly. All of them carried swords. One or two were reasonably well groomed, but the rest were ruffian-looking. The one nearest him growled in their throats and started to rise. Jiro shifted his weight, expecting a rush.

A figure by the sunken hearth in the middle of the room raised a hand. The man, clad all in dark brown clothing, sat up. He had been lying at hs ease close by the fire while a slatternly woman toasted mountain-root jelly on bamboo skewers.

'Well,' the dark-clad man called out cheerily and smiled, 'welcome, welcome!' His eyes took in Jiro's height and brawn and his smile became even more welcoming. 'You have come! How wonderful. I had been expecting to meet you. Please enter. Bring him, Kumoko.'

There was no change in the man's cheery tone, but Jiro felt menace. He started to bow, thought better of it as a skinny individual rose from the crowd, and said, 'No thank you. I believe I have made a mistake.'

The brown man smiled again. 'No! Not at all. I am only too happy you have come. Actually, I have been on the lookout for you myself. Kumoko!'

It was Jiro's training as a shipwright that saved him. The thin man threw a loop of red silk cord at him. It uncurled as it flew, and the hooks at its end tangled in Jiro's clothing. With a flick of the wrist the hojo-jutsu expert twisted the cord and made it loop around Jiro's body.

Another man would have tried to pull away or rip the cord. Jiro tried neither. He had been used to wood and ropes all his life. In several quick steps he moved to interpose a couple of wooden uprights between himself and Kumoko. The pillar stopped any further attempts to ensnare him. Pinning the silk cord to the pillar, he had enough slack to wriggle himself out of the tangle. Had he waited a second more, he would have been too tangled to move. The group of men around the fire stirred themselves in a rush. Jiro's shipwright senses came to his aid again. He seized the correct joint between pillars and roofbeams. His giant frame strained, and with a twist half the shaky roof came down.

Dry wood and straw caught fire at once. Smoke and flames burst almost at once from the structure as candles fell to the floor and the hearth fire blazed up. For Jiro it was the work of a moment to draw his sword and cut a way through the thatch. He pulled himself frenziedly through, ignoring the screams and cries of those within. He stepped out into the cold night air. From the hamlet came cries of 'Fire, fire' as the villagers organised themselves for a rescue. Jiro felt trapped. He turned wondering which way to run.

'You did me a bad turn, you bastard.' A cold, menacing voice came out of the dark. Jiro recognised the man in brown. With half his mind he wondered how the latter had got to the front of the hut so quickly. The other half was occupied by the sight of the naked blade the man carried.

'Lord Matsudaira set a price on your head. He

150

said nothing about the body. I don't think I'll send it to him.' The sword cut downwards with amazing swiftness, and Jiro barely parried. He had one chance, he realised. The other men would be emerging from the blazing hut in the next few seconds. They would not be charitable. And the villagers were on their way. He reached behind him with one hand, and threw a large handful of blazing thatch before him. The man in brown laughed contemptuously and danced back. 'More light to fight with, monster.' The straw blazed up. Without pause, using the momentary blaze of light to distract his opponent, Jiro turned and ran into the welcoming darkness.

It took him half the night to lose them. He was bruised, scratched and out of wind when he paused to drink at a small brook. He knew he was lost. Before him the brook tumbled down massive rocks and became a waterfall falling endlessly into a valley beyond. Jiro bathed his hand. One of the pursuers had almost caught him in the first few minutes of escape, and in the tussle, Jiro had received a deep cut on the left hand.

His thirst slaked, and his body slightly rested, Jiro covered his eyes with his palms. He was nearly desperate, and his belly was growling with hunger for the first time in his well-fed life. He breathed a deep breath. The sound of crickets around him stilled. Out of the darkness came a quiet, menacing voice: 'And now, samurai, you die.'

Without thinking, Jiro rolled himself over and over. The three blades that came out of the dark, aimed to hamper his movements, not kill him, flashed into the place he had been. He drew his

151

sword desperately as the man in brown cut at his head. The blades sparked in the dark with a screech. Desperately, Jiro cut at where he thought his enemy's head was. His blade hit air. He sprang to one side in panic and slashed wildly again. There was a quiet laugh some steps away. He fell and rolled, and again heard the sound of blades hitting. He wondered how many throwing spikes – shuriken – the brown man carried. He fell on a long tree branch. Unthinking he seized it and threw with all his strength. He heard the branch strike something soft, and a curse. He leaped back and heard the hum of a blade not a finger's breadth from his face. He struck and missed. A sword point struck him in a badly aimed backstroke. It scored across his belly and he felt the flash of pain. The brown man howled in triumph and leaned into his sword. He was standing awkwardly, however, and the blade stuck in Jiro's rib. Jiro tried to jump backwards, barely staggered, and his feet found air. The last thing he remembered as he fell was the sight of the brown clad man as the rays of the rising moon shone on his raised sword.

Waking was pain, and cold, and a white bearded face peering at him. Jiro could barely open his eyes. His head hurt and his eyes were puffy and swollen. Through a red haze he saw the old man was naked but for a loincloth, and dripping wet.

'Been fighting, eh?' he heard as if from a distance. 'You're a terrible samurai . . .' The rest was lost in a fog as he passed out.

'We'll never find him,' Rosamund sobbed as they toiled up a slope.

'Oh yes we will,' Okiku cheefully answered. She turned to look downhill at the perspiring blonde girl. 'This is my home, I grew up here. I never knew how much I missed it.' Her hand indicated the forested mountains, the red flash of maple leaves, the occasional wild bamboo grove. 'This is my home. If he's here, I'll find him. Give me time. But first I have to get some help, and I know precisely where.'

For the next few days they climbed up and down innumerable forest-clad slopes, or so it seemed to Rosamund, bred on easier, gentler hills. They threaded their way through a steep narrow gorge.

'Here!' the dark girl moved aside the branches of a thick bush and uncovered a faint path. They toiled up that for several hours, coming at last to a small deep saddle, almost a valley in the mountain's bosom. The floor of the saddle was covered with neat vegetable patches, most of them harvested for the winter. Hidden by a grove of trees at the other side was a small thatched cottage. Its colour blended in with the side of the mountain against which it was built. Faintly they could hear the ringing of an axe blade against wood.

Okiku drew a deep breath and tears came to her eyes. Rosamund looked at her expectantly. They had rarely talked the past days. Okiku seemed to move in a daze, shaken by memory. Once they had passed what seemed like the burned remains of a house, and Okiku had disappeared for several hours, bidding Rosamund to wait. She had returned with her face set, marked with dried tear tracks, but not a word to Rosamund. Now she seemed disposed to talk.

'This is my uncle's house. He taught me . . . my . . . craft.' Rosamund noted the hesitation. 'He was once the most powerful ninja in the world. Greater than Hattori Hanzo.' Neither the name nor the term meant anything to Rosamund.

'Now he is a yamabushi. I cannot explain . . . . A priest who lives in the mountains. Soon his knowledge will be so great he will be a buddha in life and leave us. He must undergo many austerities before he can do that, and I'm glad he hasn't succeeded yet. He knows everything that goes on in the mountains.'

An old man was sitting on the veranda that ran around the front and two sides of the house they could see. He was rapidly weaving a basket out of thin tough akebia vine. The axe was still working behind the house. He smiled at them through a flowing white beard. Thick white eyebrows over-shadowed deep eyepits. The eyes in them were hidden by shadows.

'Ah, welcome Kiku-chan. It has been some while. Your strange friend is welcome too.'

It seemed appropriate, thought Rosamund, that the old man should penetrate her disguise at once. He was dressed in white puffed trousers, tight at the calf, and a white tunic. Around his neck was a torques studded with fist-sized fuzzy balls that hung down his chest. A peculiar, tiny, multi-folded hat perched over his brow, held precariously by a thong around his head. His long white hair fell unimpeded to his shoulders.

Okiku bowed to him. 'Uncle, I am so glad to see you. I am distraught.'

154

He nodded. 'And you've also failed at the task you set for yourself: Hachiro still lives.'

She bowed again, deeper. 'Yes uncle. My sorrow betrays me'.

He nodded. 'Hachiro has been back in the mountains for a while now. I've had news of him.'

She stared at him stonily. The hated name, once loved, made her shiver. 'You could have dealt with him . . . . Or even delayed him. You knew I was coming. You know everything.'

He shook his head again, his fingers never stopping their weaving. 'No. You know I cannot act against him. I am almost ready to start on my way.' Rosamund saw Okiku blanch. 'And he will not stop me from my way. And,' he added as an afterthought, 'I have a weapon to set to his destruction. It will require some fine honing, and now that you are here, you may assist me.'

She bowed eagerly. 'I want to kill him with my own hands. I've tried, twice. Each time I failed.'

'There is a flaw in your nature. For a ninja you are too loving, too pleasure-seeking. My weapon will give you an advantage.'

'What is it?' she was again eager, scenting the kill.

'Not what, who.' He tilted his head to the sound of the chopping. 'He is a crude weapon. That is a subtle one. I've been subtle all my life; crudeness is the last thing Hachiro will expect from me. He will kill the weapon, but the weapon will kill him.' There was an unpleasant smile on the calm face, and Rosamund could see the shadow of the killer.

'Come inside and rest. I have tea.'

'No. There is a matter I must discuss with you.

155

Someone I must find, for both of us,' she indicated the silent Rosamund. 'But first I will look at your weapon.' She strode off, heading around the house.

The old man looked after her. 'A flaw in her nature. She will never be a great ninja.' He turned his attention to Rosamund. 'Foreign lady, excuse our bad manners. We are rough mountain folk. Please be seated at your ease. I will prepare some tea. I am called Ippei.' He hospitably placed a woven rush sitting-pad on the veranda.

Rosamund bowed, and said in a low voice as she seated herself. 'My name is Rosamund. It means rose,' she felt impelled to add.

'Ah, a rose and a chrysanthemum grace my hut, a year has passed,' he intoned. In more prosaic tones he added 'I will make tea.'

There was a wild feminine shriek from behind the cottage, the sound of an axe thrown down hastily, and masculine bellow.

Rosamund jumped up in terror, and Ippei's brows furrowed. Feet pounded around the other side of the cottage, accompanied by strange gurgles and moans. Ippei's fingers slid around a large gnarled staff. Had she not been watching his hands, she would not have seen the motion was so smooth.

Rosamund shrieked in surprise herself. Jiro, holding Okiku aloft with both hands, charged around the corner. He was roaring happily and shaking her. Her eyes were closed, her legs and arms wrapped around him and she moaned his name repeatedly. Tears dropped down her nose. Without letting go of Okiku he seized Rosamund and hoisted her aloft. He hugged both girls with bone-bruising strength.

It was late evening by the time they had all finished their stories.

Ippei rarely slept the night in his cottage. He wandered the forest meditating in preparation for his spirit's journey. Morning had dawned when he returned. He looked at the three entwined bodies. His gaze lingered curiously over Rosamund's white skin and full breasts. She felt his presence and awoke. She moved to cover herself, but something in his eyes stopped her. His look was detached, almost clinical rather than lustful. He gazed at her unblinkingly for a full minute. She didn't know whether to luxuriate in the minute examination or squirm under its impersonal nature.

'Interesting,' he said slowly. 'You rule with your lust. Others such as Okiku are ruled by it. You are much the stronger.'

'Oh no,' she whispered. 'Okiku is strong. She saved me . . .'

'You would have saved yourself.' He undid the ties of his trousers.

'Observe,' he commanded her. 'My body is me. It is not separate, not something that controls or is controlled.'

His short thick prick rose from a white bush. A large bag hung below. The pole rose higher, straightening until it stood like a pillar. Then, without losing its stiffness, it bent like broken reed, but only at the root. It waved to and fro for a while, and then climbed again. She looked at him with awe. It was obvious that every motion was voluntary. He sank slowly to sit cross-legged on the mat. She crept away from the tangled bodies of her friends. Her heavy breasts hung down enticingly,

157

but Ippei payed no attention. She climbed into his lap, wrapping her generous thighs around his hips. It was like embracing a warm living oak. His muscles, his prick, his bones were as hard and durable as the mountains. She moved up and down on him as he sat there contemplating infinity. She moved for what seemed like an eternity, his body remained unmoving. In frustration she dug finger-nails into his back and hips, and when that brought no response, her teeth into his chest. Neither weapon made any lasting mark on his tough leathery skin.

Whining in anger, she pummelled his chest. Exhausted, she sat on him passively, her cunt entirely occupied by his motionless prick. She felt it was the most disappointing fuck in her life. Suddenly, without moving any other part of his body, he struck. His belly muscles contracted and his thick cock, acting like a wrestler's arm, threw her backwards.

She landed, surprised, winded and pained on her behind. Without seeming to move he stood over her. Her heels were pushed over her head, her back arched. Her magnificent golden fringed mound was exposed to its full glory. Pink, glistening buttocks framed the long slit. The fat lips were compressed to narrow, long mounds.

He held her thus for a moment, and then with a motion almost too quick to follow, he slapped her once with his palm flat full against her mound. She screeched in pain and in ecstasy. Her nerve centres were filled with sensation. Her body demanded more. Before she could move, before she could indicate what it was she wanted, he rammed his prick full into her waiting, smarting cunt. The thick rod parted her gluey lips with a rush. He came into her, heading for the centres of her passion. The tip of his cock rammed hard against the soft walls of her cunt. Hard pubic bone, covered by leathery flesh, met her own soft and padded pubis. Her erect questioning clitoris was mashed painfully under the single battering thrust.

He twisted his body once, and the sensation of pain and pleasure was too much to bear. The volcano of her passion erupted once more. At the last moments, before the waves of orgasm overcame her, she managed to focus her eyes on the white haired visage above her. The dark eyes, pupils barely visible, held her in thrall. She fought against him now. She tried to contract her painfully engorged cunt, tried to squeeze the juice out of his rock-hard member. He was unyielding, and her body broke before his. Waves of pleasure engulfed her, but not before she saw his look of respect and speculation.

He rose from her before she had finished coming. She gave a satisfied gasp, and raised herself on one elbow. Okiku and Jiro were looking at her with amusement.

'Observe!' Ippei's voice was a commanding whip-lash. 'All three of you are soft. She,' he nodded in Rosamund's direction, 'is the only one who can perhaps follow me in the way. Observe me, and learn.'

His erect prick, glistening with Rosamund's juices, swayed for a moment from side to side. Then it began to wilt, until it was lying shrivelled on his thigh. Jiro, uninterested in male organs, looked appreciatively at Rosamund's dimpled back.

'Samurai!' a cold deadly voice interrupted his musings, 'you have told me you want revenge on the brown-clad man. His name is Hachiro. If you wish to live the next time you meet him, learn what I have to teach you.' The low voice was so compelling, Jiro did not notice Okiku's gasp at the sound of the name, even though Ippei sent her a reproving glance.

Again, the older man repeated 'Observe!' His flaccid prick suddenly sprang erect. To Okiku it seemed as if there were no in-between motion between flaccidity and erection. Suddenly it was there, like a fighting man's sword. Ippei's face was entirely calm and remote. The prick jerked spasmodically, and a jet of thick white cream spurted forth, drops of it hitting Rosamund's breast. Again the erect tool jerked, and another spurt leaped forth. The contraction was cut off in the middle, and the member shrivelled as rapidly as before. Jiro gaped, but Ippei's raised finger held his attention.

Again the prick rose abruptly, showered its cream forth, and subsided in mid-spasm. Ippei regarded them silently for a moment.

'A swordsman' he said in a lecturing tone, 'has his sword with him. He is not affected by his opponent's actions. A sword can be of steel, or of flesh, or best of all, of nothing. The rose knows. She carried through her intentions, though unsuccessfully, even at the moment of her triumph. You must learn to do likewise . . .'

160

CHAPTER 13

Strong hands helped him out of water that was salty
and bitter. He retched constantly. Shivers overtook
him and he would have fallen but for the hard
gentle hands that held him. A calm voice ordered
him laid down. He tried to tell them that he was
a doctor, that he needed . . . he needed . . . the
thought weaved through his mind combined with
an awful feeling of loss. The feeling of loss skipped
through his mind, to combine with a memory of
enormous granite ramparts and even greater loss.
Then all fled and he fell down into dark.

Goemon knew, by the pitching of the pallet he
was lying on, that he was in a ship. He turned his
head weakly. Nearby was an expensive pawlonia-
wood sea chest, the kind that would float if the boat
sank. There was a stir beyond the bed. A man
was sitting there, holding a bowl of tea which he
immediately offered Goemon.

'Rest now, the worst is over. You will get well
and we will talk.' Goemon sank back on the soft
pillow and closed his eyes. The slightly bitter tea
had restored him, and the movement of the ship
lulled him to a peaceful sleep.

He was out of bed by the morning of the next

161

day. The bruises and contusions he had received from being tumbled about in the giant wave of the river would ache for a while yet, but he was used to that. His belongings were all gone. He thanked his saviour.

Saizo was a tea merchant, returning to his home is Osaka from a business trip to Edo. He had just established his senior clerk there to manage a branch of his trade. In time the clerk might do well and become independent but he would always owe loyalty to his patron. For reasons he could not define, Saizo found himself liking this quiet young man he had hauled from the sea. Goemon was educated, as a doctor should be, but he possessed other branches of knowledge, had the muscles of a warrior, and harboured some hidden rage or despair in his makeup that Saizo could not readily fathom. The little Goemon wished to impart of his history came out in bits and pieces. Saizo forebore asking more probing questions. After the Osaka war, there were many men who did not wish to have their pasts revealed. Even Saizo. Particularly Saizo.

They sailed into the Yodo River port of Osaka three days after Goemon was pulled from the sea. Off to their right rose the ruin of Osaka Castle, a shadow of its former size and power, but still impressive. Goemon and Saizo were leaning on the ship rail. Goemon had been equipped with a plain cotton robe from Saizo's chest, but he still felt the loss of his staff and short sword.

'What will you do now?' asked the older man.

'Return to my trade as a doctor. If possible, I will look for my friends.'

Saizo smiled. 'I shall be returning to the tea

162

trade. An interesting occupation. I spend more time in the open air tasting tea than in the house, but even there the smell is redolent of the herb. Are you a devotee of the Tea cult?'

'I've done it . . . in the past. But I'm really not a devotee.'

'I want to spend more time at it.' The older man sighed. 'Unfortunately, the pressure of business is such . . .'

'Your establishment must be very large.'

Saizo laughed. 'No, not so large. I only started it a few years ago. Before that I was in another trade, mainly metal goods. But I came from a tea-raising family in Uji, and I knew tea very well. My two sons are doing well, but they are too young to know the business. In any case, they are city-bred and would not have the discrimination one bred in the country, such as yourself, would have . . .'

Goemon understood what Saizo was proposing. He stood staring at the bustling city of Osaka for a while. He should be heading home, he knew, but the answers he wanted still eluded him. And then there was a matter of his friends. He had tried not to think of their fate while on the ship, but perhaps here, in Osaka where they were supposed to have gone . . .

He bowed to Saizo. 'I would be grateful if you would take me on, if even for a short while, to assist you. However, I must search for my friends, you realise,' he said formally.

Saizo bent his head in agreement and smiled. 'I have some contacts along the Tokaido, and perhaps we will be able to find out more from there.'

Goemon had been working for Saizo for a month

when word came of his friends. Saizo interrupted him while he was examining a series of lined wooden boxes used to transport tea in bulk.

'I have had some news from some business acquaintances of mine near Yoshida. Two women, a nun and a pilgrim whose description fits the one you gave me, were seen there. There has since been no word, but I imagine it means they are all right.'

Goemon smiled his gratitude and rose to stretch. Saizo eyed him speculatively. Hard muscles played beneath the dark skin, and the young man bore his shoulders like one accustomed to straightening, not bowing them. The relationship between them was a peculiar one. Goemon was more than a clerk – he could read and write classical Chinese, something Saizo could not do, and would correspond for Saizo with the Chinese merchants in the city – but less than a confidant.

'I would like you to accompany me to a party tonight,' said the merchant. 'I have some business with Chinese tea merchants – I want to buy a quantity of Dragon's Well tea from Chekiang next spring – and we are finalising the deal tonight.'

Goemon bowed his assent and returned to his work. He grinned to himself wryly. The classical education he had received and against which he had struggled was proving to be of some good at last.

They rode palanquins into the Chinese quarter that night. The foods were odd, the Chinese merchants polite, remote, and oddly dressed, and there were women. Goemon had thought all foreigners alike, and he expected something like Rosamund; though, he had admitted to himself, her colour was unusual.

The men wore gowns and felt shoes. They wore soft caps even inside, in a fashion Goemon remembered as common a hundred years before his time. The women were delicate and graceful, their hair in large buns beside their ears. Tiny feet, the smallest Goemon had ever seen, peeped out from under the hems of their long dresses. He tried to see if the size of the feet was a mere illusion. Saizo caught his stare and whispered in a low voice, 'They call us barbarians, but we at least do not mutilate our women for pleasure. These women have had their feet bound since childhood.'

Goemon mused inwardly on the peculiar customs of foreigners. Oddly enough, the tiny feet gave the women a delicately swaying walk that was terrifically enticing.

The party grew noisier and happier. Puns and jokes were exchanged, largely in Chinese which Goemon and Saizo could not follow. The girls danced enchantingly. Two of them caught Goemon's eye. One was a tall, willowy creature with perfect skin and large eyes. The other, a musician, was gently playing a biwa lute while singing in a soft voice. Her lips pouted as if she disapproved of what she herself did.

'Why do they bring their own? Surely there are sufficient women in Japan?' he whispered to Saizo.

The other shook his head. 'They prefer their own. After all, one human body is much like another, it is the learned differences that count, as you well know.'

Goemon, whose pulses had quickened to the swaying movements of the tall dancer, remembered Rosamund and had to agree. He also remembered

165

that he had not had a woman for a month. A Chinese merchant caught his eye. He was a roly-poly man who had played a major part in the earlier negotiations.

'I see our little flowers attract your fancy. Displanted, they are somewhat wilted, but still retain some of their charm. I am sorry we have nothing better to offer. I notice you have been regarding the dancer and the little plump accompanist . . .' he said.

'I was wondering about their feet,' answered Goemon truthfully.

'Ah,' said the other in his badly accented Japanese. 'You like the flying swallows. I must say that I find the bare feet of your women rather unattractive. Well, you shall have both of them, and we can discuss their virtues later.'

He called the dancer to him. After a short whispered conversation, she bowed to Goemon and led him from the room. Other men too were leaving.

She led him to a small room. In it was a waist-high platform overlooking a tiny garden. The platform was laid with a single large pallet. A tea service was within reach. She bowed to him. He slipped a hand into her gown. There was a fabric barrier between his hand and her full breasts. Impatiently he opened her dress. A red-embroidered breast-band covered her from breasts to thighs. He slipped the dress off her shoulders and dropped it to the floor, then stood back. She gazed at him with a calm face as if amused at his impetuosity.

She had long legs of an ivory white colour. She wore white socks on her feet and tiny red felt slippers. The red breast-band hid her body and breast from view. Her neck was long and pale too. She leaned forward and licked him slowly and sensuously on the lips. The tip of her tongue barely penetrated his parted lips, darted in and withdrew again.

He searched with his hand for the ties of the breast-band, then impatiently pushed it down from her tits. There was momentary resistance, then the large tits popped free. He grasped them hungrily, squeezing the soft dropping flesh and caressing the nipples with his thumbs. She pushed him away gently and raised the breast-band to expose her cunt, then pushed him down onto a high backed chair.

He sat down and licked his lips. With a swaying motion forced on her by her tiny feet, she floated across the room. Her full-moon buttocks moved in an undulating motion exquisite to watch. She bent over to pick up a small tabouret, and Goemon could see the length of her long legs, a long-lipped cunt, and taut muscles that hid the tiny hole of her ass. He was in less of a hurry now, more in control of his desire, and he knew all of those things were for him.

She picked up the tabouret and carried it across the room. Her full, rather droopy breasts swayed with every twist of her hips. She placed the tabouret before his chair and placed her left foot on it. Her cunt was long and thin. The inner lips projected a bit beyond the outer, and it was fringed very lightly with black hair.

She let him enjoy the sight for a while, then her hand stole downwards, caressing his lower belly as it came. Like a snake flowing down a branch, the boneless-seeming motion fascinated him. The tip of her middle finger reached the uppermost reach of her crevice and stopped. He took a deep breath waiting for her act to continue. She slid her finger down the length of her crack and then on to her thigh. The digit emerged shiny with her inner moisture. The lips had parted gently before the passage, but hid the pink-coral interior. The hand rose up again through the same path. This time middle finger was joined by ring, and the crack widened enough to show pink flesh glistening with love's tears. This time she paused with the tips of her fingers resting on the tiny, invisible nub of her clitoris. She blinked, slowly and languorously, once, then her hand descended again, the two fingers joined by the index. She slid them down to the middle of her long slit, and stopped. The tips of all three fingers were hidden in the folds of her flower-like cunt. Gently, she spread ring and index fingers and moved middle finger out of the way. Her entire cunt lay exposed to Goemon's eyes. White outer skin, black fringe, and pink-going-into-deeper-coral channel greeted him. He could feel his prick as rock-hard fire between his legs.

She peered at him through half-closed eyelids. The foot on the tabouret rose, and she pivoted on her right leg. The tiny gilded foot came to rest on the mound in his clothing. She applied more pressure, and he moved against it. She leaned forwards slightly and the enticing view of her cunt was only a foot from his eyes. He forebore to touch, and raised his eyes to look at her face. She wore a look of approval for his civilised forbearance.

She diddled him slowly and thoroughly with her

foot. Nothing showed on her face, and Goemon could not know that she was disappointed he did not caress the foot, squeezing it onto his member. By now, however, he was in a state of excitement that was irrevocable. With the hand that was not holding open her flower, she fumbled with his robe. She flipped it aside, then eased the folds of his loincloth. Involuntarily his hands rose and softly stroked the lower surface of her breasts that hung like inviting pink-tipped fruit before his face.

His erection leaped free like a lance. She swayed back still on one leg and pivoted to place her foot on the ground, ass to him. Her left hand supported her on the tabouret while her right still held herself open. Her smooth creamy backside peeked back at him. The tiny starfish of her asshole, hidden till now, beckoned, but below it lay a hole swimming with the honey he craved. She pushed herself back until her open lips hovered barely touching the tip of his prick.

She called out something in Chinese, and the biwa player, fully dressed, floated into the room. Her pouting lips were more prominent, and Goemon could now see she was a small, plump girl, a delicate contrast to the dancer. The Biwa player approached the couple. She supported the dancer's shoulders as the latter eased herself slowly down onto Goemon's prick.

The trip up her channel seemed to take forever. Goemon strove to restrain himself from pushing forward with all his strength. The head of his rampant cock separated the narrow channel, gliding up to the heat inside. The collar of his shaft seemed clasped by a warm, infinitely soft gloved hand.

At last their hairs met. The dancer still bore all of her weight on her legs and hand. The other hand delicately fingered Goemon's balls and her own lips at the same time. She turned her head to stare at him, smiled, and then suddenly collapsed, relaxing all her muscles and applying all her strength to constricting her cunt. The other girl looked at him expectantly.

Instinctively, Goemon knew what was expected of him. He rammed forward from his seat with one tremendous thrust. He would not need many shoves before he came. In fact he needed but three. The smaller girl supported the other by her shoulders against the onslaught. He rammed furiously, and suddenly his sperm rose from his balls in an uncontrollable stream. Spurt followed spurt as his legs trembled, trying to hold him. He clawed at her ass and thighs, and then his full weight fell on her as he died in final spasms. He raised himself heavily from his near-faint. The two girls, motionless, were waiting for his recovery. He stepped back, his still-erect cock impeding his motions. With a shrug of his shoulders he dropped his robe and his loosened loincloth. The two looked at him in approval.

The biwa player knelt before Goemon, ran her lips around the tip of his dripping prick, then pushed her head forward until the length of his shaft disappeared between her lips and down her throat. Gently, so as not to hurt his super-sensitive member, she sucked the length, and then withdrew, swallowing the salty-sour juices.

'I Peach Blossom,' she said in broken Japanese. 'She Willow Girl. Now you not so full, we do properly.'

She stripped the red breast-band off Willow and removed her own clothes. They were both now naked from ankle to hair. Neither removed her feet coverings nor her hair ornaments. Idly, while watching, Goemon wondered if the hairpins were sharp steel spikes – the dancing woman's protection – that local dancing women wore.

The two girls stood for a moment side by side. Peach Blossom, in contrast to Willow Girl, was short and plump. She had flat wide breasts with darker nipples. Her bush was a bit more luxurious, and her hips wider than the other's. Her pouting lips were complemented by the lips of her cunt; fleshy and protuberant, they reminded Goemon of Rosamund, except that the clitoris was invisibly tiny, hidden in the folds.

Willow lay back on the pallet and spread her legs, then raised her knees to her breast. Peach laid herself down on the inviting figure. She rubbed her tits slowly, then faster against Willow. The two girls' nipples danced and pushed together. Willow raised her head slightly, and Peach kissed her deeply and long. Then she gently lowered herself onto the other, fitting the lips of her cunt onto the taller girl's. The two long mounds met in a squashy kiss. Goemon lowered himself on the tabouret and enjoyed the sight.

Like two goldfish kissing in water, the two cunts met in a symmetrical kiss. Willow's longer interior lips were mashed by the weight of the other girl. They spread themselves and there was a slick, sliding movement as the two moved their hips slightly. Goemon stuck forth his hand and laid it between the lips. His finger was surrounded on four sides by wonderfully slithery, rubber-soft woman flesh. Willow smiled at him in approval at his tempered and cultured approach. He withdrew his fingers and brought his face closer to smell the musk. The girls' cunts smelled different, he knew, but the differences in perfume were so slight he could not tell which scent came from which glistening orifice.

He withdrew his head, and watched the writhing of the two alabaster figures on the bed. Peach turned her head, and her hand that had been on Willow's shoulder took hold of his erect member. She drew him gently towards her. She positioned the broad head of his tool between the four lips of their joined cunts. He waited for the next move. The two bodies continued undulating one on the other. Tiny tremors were transmitted from their slick lips to his hard cock.

'Now!' commanded Peach. He thrust his cock forward and it slid slickly between the two girls. The sensation was like nothing he had ever felt before. The lips were slick but they were rougher than the orifice of a cunt. The hair fringe scraped along the length of his throbbing prick, roughly massaging the skin, scrubbing it in the foam produced from the girls' labial folds. Willow and Peach continued their pressure on one another, squeezing his willing staff between them.

He let his hands roam freely on their bodies. He felt the difference between Willow's muscular thighs and Peach's softly rounded ones. He scratched along their flanks, gently at first, then in a frenzy. The two girls he heard were murmuring softly, whether endearments to one another or to himself, he neither knew nor cared. The rising and falling tones of the language met the rhythm of their three bodies and encouraged the force of their movements.

Sooner than he had expected, his cock started throbbing in the incipient moments of orgasm. He seemed to swell, and felt as it he would burst. Peach's hand had been holding the base of his prick all this time. As she felt the slight tightening of his cock, the stiffening of his body, she dug her thumb hard into the base of his cock. The pain was exquisite, and he gasped with its intensity. His urge to shoot his load between the two bodies receded. Annoyed, he was about to slap the plump ass in front of him. She looked at his face.

'Gentleman no finish and waste self so soon. So stop now.'

He stepped back, expectant now, and the two girls rolled apart. Willow rose and hugged him close. She led his hand the length of her sopping cunt, then drew Peach close and repeated the movement in her friend. She turned and made him sit on the bed, close to the edge, leaning her head on his shoulder so he could see Peach. The plump lute player swayed forward and fetched the small tabouret. She placed it before him. Turning her back and leaning on the tabouret, she impaled herself swiftly on his rearing manhood. Her cunt was softer than Willow's, he decided. Her plump buttocks did not dig into his thighs the way the thinner girl's had. Willow raised her leg and threw it over the other girl's back like a rider mounting a horse, but without losing her hug of Goemon.

Her fingers scratched at his back and neck gently, and she kissed him passionately.

Leaning on the tabouret, Peach raised and lowered her plump rump. Willow kissed his neck, nibbled at his shoulder. She stuck her tongue into his mouth, and he reciprocated, driving his labial member deeply into the warm sucking cavern. His cock was being massaged rapidly by Peach, who then added a sideways swirl every time she felt the stiff hairs at the base of his arrow touch her delicate ass.

Goemon's hands were free to roam. Willow's breasts hung temptingly before his hands. He squeezed her viciously as he used to do to Rosamund. She moved protestingly and her kisses lost their vigour and delicacy. He desisted and caressed, then squeezed them gently and her touch on his skin improved. He ran his hand lightly down her slim muscular back, down the base of her spine. He parted her buns and fingered the tiny puckered asshole. He remembered Peach, whose cunt riding him was giving him such pleasure. He wished to push himself into her, but Willow's embrace held him hard on his seat. He slid his hand down and smoothed the plump jiggly fat of her ass. Peach looked at him over her shoulder.

'Scratch the starfish,' she said.

Through gasps and the pressure of Willow's lips he said, 'What?'

'Scratch the starfish!' she repeated. One hand slipped back and she forced his digit into her tiny bud.

Understanding flooded him. He rammed his fore-finger home into her welcoming asshole. She sighed in satisfaction. The taut muscular ring relaxed reluctantly and his rigid finger slide greasily into her welcoming depths. He slid his other hand down Willow's back and fingered her rear hole for a moment. She bit him slightly, then nibbled passionately at his ear. He thrust himself inside, and she gasped with pleasure. Forcefully, he began ramming his fingers into the two girls. They both moaned with expectant pleasure. The rhythm of their actions increased. Peach rammed herself hard down on him. Suddenly she stiffened. Her bottom quivered and the quiver spread to the rest of her. She moaned incoherently and her cunt flooded the length of his prick as she came. Willow, feeling her friend's climax, pushed back against his finger. He spread his hand and his other fingers played busily the length of her juice-filled cunt. She stiffened and moaned. Her tongue moved like a trip-hammer into his ear. She bit it painfully as the climax finally hit her.

Goemon felt he was about to explode. He thrust with all his might upwards. The two girls held him down. Willow's hand sneaked down to the base of his lust-driven prick, and squeezed hard. There was a buzzing in his ears and his body shook with the sudden effort, but the need to explode was gone. He wondered how long he would be able to keep this up.

The girls seemed to have no doubt as to his ability. They disentangled themselves. Willow curled herself round Goemon as he sat. Her left foot thrust between his thighs to hold them open. Curling in marvellous flexibility, she pressed her belly and tits against his back and hips. She rested

her cheek on his right thigh, and started tonguing
him slowly the length of his softening prick. The
movements of her delicate wet tongue soon
returned his prick to life. He looked down at the
black-haired head, and the buns of hair above her
ears bounced with the movement of her head.

Peach glided across the room and disappeared
behind a screen. He watched her move with
pleasure at the swaying motion. Willow transferred
her attentions to his hair-sprouting sack, and he
shivered with the sensation. Somewhat like eating
poisonous blowfish; exquisite pleasure and the tinge
of danger.

Peach reappeared with a tray and a flute. She fed
him candied fruits and nuts of strange taste –
ginger, dates, apples – and a fiery yellow wine. He
poured a cup for her, and she drank it daintily.
Then a cup for Willow, who stopped her ministrations to his prick long enough to sip. While she
drank, Peach bent forward and engulfed the head
of his member with her soft mouth. She had kept
some of the liquor on her tongue, and it burned
fiercely but pleasantly as she sucked.

Willow uncoiled herself from around him and he
stepped to the floor. The two girls heaped some
bolsters on the bed, and she lay down again, facing
him, her back raised by the bolsters. She raised her
legs together vertically without effort. The sight
was enchanting. Her long slim legs tapered to the
tiny red-shod feet above. Her long narrow cunt was
forced forward between her tightly pressed legs. It
made a long fleshy channel, barely fringed by black
hair.

Peach led him forward by his rampant manhood.

She guided him into Willow's expectant cunt. She was as tight as a virgin. The head of his cock could barely make it past the pressure exerted by her strong dancer's legs, which she held apparently without any effort. She smiled at him as he seized her around the waist and with a mighty shove inserted himself as far as he could. He was stopped from full insertion by Peach's fist that held his staff tight. The plump girl drew him out slowly until only the point was touching Willow's hole. Using the tip, she began stroking the length of the taller girl's fleshy mound. She lingered occasionally at the entrance to the tightly squeezed opening and at the barely seen clitoris. Willow began to whine excitedly. Peach poised his prick at the entrance, and again he plunged up the gluey channel, only to be stopped by Peach's fist. She drew him out again. Willow's face was contorted with lust, and her full tits quivered with tension, but her legs remained as tightly joined as before.

Drawing him out again, Peach repeated the movement. The pauses between insertion grew shorter. Willow's almond eyes closed. Sweat beaded her face and she was now quivering violently and uncontrollably. Finally, as he was inserting against Willow's renewed resistance, she withdrew her hand. Unrestrained except by the tightness of Willow's thighs, Goemon's cock plunged the full length of the reclining girl's cunt. Peach twined herself about him, her slick cunt leaving snail-trails of her juices on his thigh.

He felt the depths of Willow's cunt as he rammed fiercely into her. She gave a high-pitched scream, and her reserves broke as she came. Her legs waved wildly in the air, twining themselves around his neck, then loosening as spasm after spasm took her. She repeated her moan, lower pitched now, and her lids opened on unfocusing eyes.

He tried to join her in her climax, thrusting into her again. Peach pushed against him forcefully, and he almost slipped out of the dancer's body. Peach squeezed his prick hard with one hand, while the other dug into the spot at its base. His urge subsided once more. This time he was angry. He would have turned and struck the plump girl, but was stopped by her actions. Unhurriedly she bent over and gently touched his inflamed tool with her lips. She pulled him fully out of Willow, who now had pulled her legs down so that her feet rested on Peach's shoulders. Peach licked the overflowing cunt of her friend, then she raised her head and positioned the tip of Goemon's wet cock at the entrance to the dancer's hole. Without losing her hold on his cock, she circled him with her arms. Her flat tits pushed into her back and the fur between her thighs brushed his ass. She let go of his manhood, and laid her palms flat against the other girl's buns. The dancer looked at him entreatingly.

Gently he inserted the broad head of his cock into the waiting hole. Willow's face was contorted with lustful anticipation. The flange of his cock's head slipped inside and she gasped. He sank further in. The tightness was almost painful, and he knew that this time there would be no stopping him. She gave a shudder and a loud sigh when his hairs tickled her ass. He pulled back a bit and then began ramming into her with short movements. She

178

sighed contentedly. He played with her exposed cunt, sliding his fingers up and down the slick lips, teasing the tiny pearl of her clit.

His strokes grew stronger, and she writhed in pleasure. He played with her full breasts, mashed by the power of her legs, and slid a finger into her mouth where she bit it softly. When his hand came back to her stretched cunt he found Peach's little fingers were gambolling amidst the folds. Willow approached her climax. She chewed at her lip and her eyes seemed to glaze. This time there was no stopping him. He felt he would kill to let his sperm spurt out. He rammed himself powerfully into the moaning girl as the biwa player licked and kissed his back.

She came with a rush. This time she retained her senses. Muscles that she had kept in reserve came into action. Her anus contracted forcefully, squeezing the pleasure-making machine inside. Goemon felt his cock was being cut off. The stream of jism, when it came, was accompanied by pain, but also by the most explosive spurt of pleasure he had ever felt. His cock, independent of his collapsing body, shot load after load into the dancer's depths, and he collapsed across her supine body.

He lay at ease on the bed, and the two girls bathed his cock and balls with warm scented towels. When he had recovered, they stroked his muscular body innocently with their hands. Their trained fingers massaged tired muscles, avoiding his cock. They ate a light meal of noodles and broiled eel. The two girls brought the tabouret close to the side of the bed. Peach Blossom lay down and spread her legs wide. She leaned against the bolsters and played traditional airs with her flute. Willow opened the paper-paned windows onto a tiny garden housing pots of golden chrysanthemums. The flowers reminded Goemon of his lost friends and he sighed at the memory. Recognising his mood, Peach played soft country tunes. He studied her plump cunt with appreciation, stroking her legs occasionally.

Willow stood behind him, massaging his shoulders. Now she pressed her full tits into his back. The erect nipples dug into his skin like little fingers. She slid her hand across his stomach and played with the hair at its base. His prick began responding, rolling about on his thigh. She wiped her fingers through Peach's open cunt, and anointed him with the moisture. His prick rose to fullness.

The dancer urged him forward onto her friend. She supported him and aimed his cock into Peach's waiting hole. This time he needed no controlling hand. He fucked slowly, controlling himself not to come. Peach continued playing her flute the while. The airs became breathier and faster as she approached her climax. She made the instrument sing her passion and delight, and when she came, her plump body quivering, the music died down with a long quivering sigh.

Willow had been kissing and fondling Goemon's ass the while. Her hands had been busy holding and caressing Goemon's stone bag, occasionally dipping into the musician's sopping cunt. As soon as Peach has come, she slapped Goemon roughly on the ass. Startled, he lost his concentration. His body rammed forward powerfully. Peach Blossom gave a squeak and the flute dropped from her lips. Letting himself go, Goemon clawed her rounded buttocks. She raised her legs and hugged him around the body. Her hands clawed at his back. He rammed himself furiously into her gluey crack. His sperm began to rise again. He ground his hips hard against the yielding surface of her fat thighs. Willow slapped his ass in encouragement. He came with a bellow, twisting his body from side to side like a hooked fish. Peach gasped and came with him, her face contorted and her lips pouting.

He lay on the velvet soft couch of her body for a while. Willow said something in Chinese. The two girls rolled him onto the bed. He lay flat on his back. Willow straddled his head. Her cunt hung before his face. He stuck out a questing stiff tongue and was rewarded by a quiver. Moisture ran down her thigh. She leaned forward and engulfed his flaccid sopping prick in her mouth. The whole of his member disappeared down that questing furnace. It stiffened somewhat, and she withdrew her head until her lips encircled only the purple hood of his rod. Peach kissed Willow's face and eyes, and then sucked softly at the now-thickening shaft. Her tongue played a tattoo on the veined surface, and she hummed a light tune.

Goemon's recovery was almost immediate. He began tonguing the tall girl's exquisite cunt. She moaned happily.

'Harder, harder, she wants,' said Peach hurriedly, then returned to her own task.

He dug his tongue into the expectant cunt and was rewarded with a flood of juice. His hands roved over the dancer's body, and when Peach moved over to parallel his body, she too received her share from his hands on her sopping cunt, running with both their juices.

His cock returned to full erection. Peach swung herself over him and impaled herself. She began a vigorous rocking motion interspersed with raising and lowering her body the full length of his rod. He thrust himself upwards to meet her descending weight. Willow rubbed her cunt heavily over his mouth until he thought he'd suffocate. Suddenly Peach dropped her full weight on his cock. He rammed himself furiously upwards. Her thighs clenched as she came.

The girls switched places. He licked at Peach Blossom's gooey cunt, her hairs tickling his mouth and chin. Willow faced the plump girl and passionately kissed her on the lips. Her hands pulled at the soft flesh. She pushed Peach away until the plump girl's body was arched backwards, her tits stretched flat. Lowering her head she kissed Goemon and Peach Blossom's cunt simultaneously. The action of her tongue on the other girl's clit and the thrust of her tongue into Goemon's mouth made his own body begin to jerk in rhythm with her. He dug his hand deep into her willing asshole, his other busily pinching Peach Blossom's nipples.

All three of them came at the same moment. Goemon suffocating for air pushed the plump girl away from his face. Willow Girl rolled off his exhausted prick. The last thing he saw before falling asleep was the peaceful face of Willow Girl as she idly fondled his flaccid member.

CHAPTER 14

The months of winter had been the hardest of Jiro's life. He had practised incessantly with his sword, with a sword in either hand, standing on logs, in freezing water to his waist, dangling by his feet from a rope. He practised with blunt wooden staves against Okiku, and with a naked live blade against Ippei's gnarled staff. The staff struck him constantly, but his blade never even nicked his white-haired tormentor.

Sometimes Jiro was too tired for sex. It seemed to him that that was precisely the time Ippei would pick for an orgy. The older man seemed to have as inexhaustible a lust as the three younger people. Unlike Jiro, however, he seemed unaffected by the strenuous exercise.

In the midst of winter, Jiro was woken by Ippei before the stars had left the sky. Come, the old man motioned with his head. Jiro searched sleepily for his clothes, but a light blow of the staff on his hand stopped him. He grabbed his sword, and followed Ippei naked into the light snow cover that had fallen. Ippei set a stiff pace, and Jiro had no time to shiver, though cold gusts of wind cut into his skin.

They climbed out of the protective saddle and the wind struck Jiro with a thousand knives. After a while he began to hear the sound of a waterfall. They rounded the shoulder of a mountain. Before them was a small pool. A waterfall fell, unfrozen, into the pool which was rimmed with ice. The water hit a flat rock and sprayed to all sides, booming and splashing as it fell.

'The time has come for you to learn swordsmanship. Or die. You can no longer amuse yourself playing with swords of all kinds. You must become a swordsman if you are to survive your next meeting with Hachiro.' He motioned Jiro into the pool. The water cut like knives. His feet lost sensation almost immediately. Jiro sat himself on the flat rock. The water from the waterfall was warmer by several degrees that the pool, but it still chilled him. It pounded on his head and shoulders, ran down his body. The effort to sit still brought dark shadows before his eyes, and he thought he would become sick. Impassively, Ippei stood on the bank leaning on his staff and watched the immobile youth while the sun rose.

Ippei walked off awhile after dawn. He returned after a while, carrying a basket. He slowly built a small fire, and placed a sake bottle in the embers. The contrast between his own miserable condition and Ippei's finicky pleasures drove Jiro frantic. Grimly he hung onto the last shards of his resolve, and sat immobile. Ippei delicately sipped at his wine until it was all gone. The ludicrous nature of the situation began to penetrate Jiro's fozen consciousness. He almost laughed aloud at the contrast between Ippei's lolling on the bank and

184

his own frozen posture. The older man rose, and motioned him out from under the waterfall.

The walk back was an agony. Cold winds cut into Jiro's exposed body. Ippei chattered at him inconsequentially, and insisted on stopping time after time to point out the view or a particularly lovely snow-covered tree. Jiro collapsed into the bedding in the house, but was almost immediately aroused by Ippei's demands for innumerable petty chores.

The girls stole worried glances at Jiro, who felt he was near collapse. The day wore on. After a light meal, they lay down again. Again Jiro was awakened and he followed Ippei to the waterfall. Again he sat there, under the freezing shower. This time Ippei produced a pot of warm stew, and regaled himself with it calmly while Jiro, body erect, hands in lap, bore the brunt of the waterfall.

A third day repeated the same pattern. Ippei amused himself by pelting Jiro with chips of ice. He insisted Jiro avoid the missiles without using his hands or moving from his seat. By twisting his body frantically, Jiro managed to avoid some of the ice. By day's end he was covered with cuts, and was so tired that he could not sleep. Four days continued in the same pattern. Jiro felt he was near death. He could barely avoid the missiles thrown at him, which now included large rocks. Once, when he was too slow, Ippei actually threw a knife, which he later insisted Jiro retrieve from the pool where it had sunk.

The morning of the eighth day dawned. Okiku and Rosamund, their eyes half closed, watched as Jiro staggered to his feet in the dark. Ippei loomed over them all. Jiro's eyes barely functioned, and notwithstanding his strength, he staggered as he wove a ragged pace behind Ippei. He sat in the pool and his mind ceased to function. His body automatically tried to avoid the missiles thrown by Ippei, some of which hit his lacerated frozen skin painfully. The rain of thrown missiles stopped. Jiro saw Ippei disappear into the forest, and he wondered dully what new torment the old man would think of.

The thud of a shard of ice on his skin brought him to full consciousness. He avoided the casually thrown missiles drunkenly. Ippei was busy. He built a lean-to, and layered its floor comfortably with a reed mat he had brought. He built a small fire and set some sake to warm in the ashes. Jiro watched the preparations dully. His forces were ebbing, and only his stubbornness kept him in place.

Ippei's preparations were complete, and he disappeared once again into the forest. Okiku and Rosamund were with him when he returned. They cast no glance in his direction. It was still dark in the shadows of the cliff, and the motionless figure in the pool could have been any other rock.

The three on land made themselves comfortable in the lean-to. Ippei ran his eyes, then his hands, over the figures of the two girls. The contrast between the lush blonde and the slim dark girl pleased him. He flipped Rosamund's skirts aside, and laid her on her back. His prick felt as cold as ice at first, but it warmed up very quickly once it was buried in her fur. Rosamund wriggled with pleasure. Snow began falling, but the warmth generated by the old man lying on her, the sake she drunk, and Okiku lying at her side and caressing her breasts gently, made her enjoy the weather. Soon she began to feel the familiar waves of pleasure rise in her. She turned to Okiku and slid a hand onto the inviting large-nippled breasts. Okiku pushed against the warm soft hand, rubbing her painfully-erect nipples against the pressure. She wished Jiro were with them. She worried about the poor man. Ippei had been driving the young giant hard, and he had become so tired her cunt was aching for the presence of his loved cock.

Ippei rammed heavily into Rosamund for awhile. She enjoyed the sensation, but the old man, while an excellent fucker, rarely supplied her with the sensations she really craved. She imagined herself in Goemon's arms. She wished he were hitting her, striking her erect nipples, biting the lips of her cunt, forcing himself roughly into her. Images of what he would do and had done to her danced in her brain. Her back arched with the thought. Her robe loosened and Ippei pushed it almost completely off. The biting cold was a welcome sensation to the blonde. Her fair skin felt the pinches of snow particles. Goose bumps rose on her fair breasts and she squeezed the nipples hard.

Ippei looked into her eyes. There was something demanding in her eyes, something he knew he could not properly supply. She grinned at him fiercely through her pleasure. Her cunt contracted roughly on his prick. He fought back, ramming himself in deeper. She smiled again, happily this time. Her cunt muscles clenched like a might fist. Ippei felt the pain, and pushed in with the force he would have used stabbing with a knife. He reached the depths of her cunt, beating against the soft walls of her cervix. The blunt head of his stiff splitting pole undoubtedly caused her pain, but it only made her contract her cunt muscles the more. The sensation of velvety, wet smoothness was still there, but it was encased in the power of a muscular fist that threatened his being. He looked into her face and saw, through the pain and the pleasure that chased one another there, the glint of victory. He tried the trick he had used in their first fuck. His muscles contracted explosively and his power shot her forward, off his pole. This time however her muscles contracted in time with his own. The broad flange of his cock was caught by her powerful grip. He was trapped in her, and her beautiful red lips gave him a full smile that blazed like a rose through the snow.

Ippei used his last resort. He had not been a successful ninja – a master of the arts of escape – for nothing. His balls constricted and the tip of his prick gushed spurts of white slick come. He inundated the insides of Rosamund's cunt. He thrust forward at the same moment. Rosamund, caught unawares, felt the thrills of her own climax and she shuddered. Her cunt muscles contracted with each thrill, but this time the added slickness of her spermed insides could not hold on to the old man's living poker, and he escaped. She laughed wryly up at him, and he joined her.

'Very good. Very good,' he said.

He slipped off her and disrobed her completely. The cold smote unnoticed through the warmth of her exercise. Ippei turned to Okiku, who had been amusing herself by rubbing Rosamund's hands in her own crack, waiting her turn, and said 'Now, do as I told you.' Outside their shelter the snow continued falling on the forest and the pond. The waterfall fell unceasing on its rocks, hidden from view by the sheets of white.

Ippei lay on his back. He raised Rosamund by her hips and seated her on his mouth. His wonderfully long and active tongue played with the slick lips of her moistened cunt. He licked, then sucked her prominent clitoris. She sighed pleasurably, but he knew now that did not satisfy her. Taking a length of his beard, he wrapped it one half turn around the cheeky fleshy digit. He sawed it back and forth causing a sensation she had never felt before. she bounced rapidly on his face, intent on getting the most out of it. Beside them Okiku fumbled in the gloom, stripping her clothes off.

Rosamund leaned forward. Her full red lips engulfed the man's erect cock. She wetted it copiously with her tongue. Then she began a long slow sucking movement. She forced the cock down her mouth until it touched her tonsils, then withdrew it till the tip was almost past her lips. She used her teeth delicately, aware that not all shared her pleasures, and nipped the loose skin of the rod's bottom side. She began panting in-between times as the sensation of Ippei's beard on her cunt penetrated deeper into her body, and she swayed from side to side to deepen the penetration of his tongue.

Okiku shoved Rosamund's head roughly aside and eased herself gently down on the waiting fleshy sword. Entranced, Rosamund watched the thick

189

rod cleave a way up the dark lips, bending them inwards, and disappear inside her friend's waiting hole. The white and black hairs joined. Rosamund licked the juncture and butted against the joined muscular bellies. She watched again as Okiku raised herself on the rod. The lips clung to the prick like a pursed mouth reluctant to let go of its prey. The action was repeated, the rhythm kept her constant, though now Okiku added a shake at the bottom of her arc.

Wishing to change the view, Rosamund raised her head to kiss her friend's lips. She sat erect, Ippei's tongue darting into her pursed asshole and then her cunt in lightning thrusts. She saw Okiku's slim body, dark sharp nipples erect on small golden coloured breasts, hands resting on Ippei's chest. Then she saw Okiku's face and screamed. At the sound of the scream, Ippei, his head still buried between Rosamund's thighs, seized the staff that lay beside him. There was a click, and the tip of the staff flew off. From the corner of her eye Rosamund saw a foot of polished steel emerge. Without aiming, Ippei threw the lance into the dark, in the direction of the waterfall.

Jiro knew death was approaching. The cold water had numbed his arms and legs; the constant drumming of the waterfall on his head and shoulders had numbed his thinking. He could not raise a conscious thought, could not muster the energy or the personal will to save himself. Vaguely he knew that the pain and the cold were killing him. He faced death calmly, not as a samurai was supposed to, with courage, but in a completely detached manner. The knowledge of death from cold and exhaustion was there tangibly, and he accepted it as passively as a cherry blossom falling to the ground.

There was a scream from the lean-to shelter before him which he barely heard. It was followed by a hissing sound. The world seemed to slow, almost stop. He was conscious of every drop of water in the waterfall. The stone he sat on achieved an individuality and presence it never had before. Every tree, every bush he saw stood out with preternatural clarity. Facing him came sudden death. The steel shining lancehead was almost a pinpoint. He saw with great clarity that it would intersect his middle, pinning him helplessly to the rock. There was no way he could avoid death. Unthinking, something inside him took over. A toughness he had never been aware of, had never been called on to use grabbed him by the scruff of the neck. Unconsciously, his belly expanded, balancing his self-hood in a point above his loins.

The lance hissed by while Jiro, his legs still crossed under him, leaped into the air from a sitting position. He landed crouching on the rock. With a second leap he crossed the length of the small pool in the direction of the three figures in the lean-to. Rosamund's blonde-framed face stared at him with open round eyes and mouth. Ippei's head was hidden beneath her thighs. A third, slim, familiar figure was crouched in Ippei's hips. He leaped towards them. The figure turned its head and he faced a demon.

Bulbous staring eyes, the eybrows somehow expressing horror and sorrow at once, stared at him. The mouth was open in a snarling sneer. Gold

191

capped teech were bared, ready to bite. Two bone-white horns projected forward from the forehead.

He leaped forwards in delirium, and grabbed the demon's muscular slim shoulders. He had only one weapon with him. As the demon bowed its head away from him, he stabbed into her with all his might.

Okiku, her cunt full of Ippei's prick, felt the sudden forceful stab of Jiro's violent penetration. His huge prick that had delighted her at all times punched painfully into her already extended love channel. She howled in pain as Jiro forced his way unthinking up her. The two pricks seemed to struggle in her, one fighting to escape, the other to stab her to her vitals. Jiro's hands on her shoulders, that were so welcome, scraped icily down and grasped roughly at her breasts. his huge fists clenched, and she groaned at the pain of it. She tried to struggle, to avoid this rough treatment, but the power of her lover held her immobile. Meanwhile his enormous cock was tearing at her cunt. His teeth descended to her neck, ready to rend, when Ippei reached out and loosened the ties of her demon mask. Her face contorted with pain turned to Jiro. His frenzy subsided, and he looked at her in bewilderment. Suddenly she was conscious that Ippei's prick had dwindled, and was pulling out of her. The pain disappeared, and the loneliness of the past few days without Jiro's loving thrusts in her cunt returned.

'Please, please lover. Don't stop. Don't stop at all. Do it any way you want. Please fuck me, fuck me hard . . .' she moaned.

Obligingly, Jiro began the long and pleasurable

192

strokes she so loved. His hands caressed her back-side and hips enticingly. He drove his now-gentle fingers into the crack of her pussy, trailing slime up her belly and circling her nipples. His mouth covered first one ear and then the next, and his cock never stopped its pounding rhythm into her grateful cunt. She moaned ecstatically. This was what she wanted, this was what she had missed. She bowed supinely and passively before him, her hands flat on the ground, her slim ass jerking in the air, arching herself for the pleasure of them both.

Ippei and Rosamund looked on. Rosamund was happy for her friend. This, she knew, was what Okiku had waited for. The gentle woman was some-thing new, a side of her friend she had not seen. In time, she knew, she too would enjoy that massive cock, but in the meantime she was content to watch.

Ippei watched with much less approval. He shook his white head. 'A flawed ninja. This one will never be great. My training of her is to no avail. At least the man will serve my purpose.' He sighed. His own cycle was coming to a close, as was this chapter of history.

As the couple on the ground reached their inevi-table climax in shudders and soft cries of pleasure, the snow stopped. Ippei bent over Jiro. 'You are ready now, warrior,' he said.

CHAPTER 15

Saizo bent over a gnarled dwarf plum tree. It was in full bloom and the red of the blossoms stood in contrast to his sombre dress and Goemon's sombre mood.

The months of winter had been hard on the young man. He did his duties conscientiously and well, and demonstrated a good knowledge of tea, and a growing knowledge of marketing and selling. He brought to these latter accomplishments a natural intelligence, and a training in the use of abacus and writing brush. No news had come of his friends, and he was anxious to search for them himself. And the atmosphere of the merchant's shop, congenial though it may have been, was not what he had been used to.

'Please do me a favour, Goemon-san,' said Saizo suddenly, interrupting Goemon's accounting. 'I must soon go to Uji, to see about the new crop.' Uji tea was the best in the islands. 'I would be grateful if you could carry some messages to merchants in Miyako for me. It will also be an opportunity for you to visit that graceful city.'

Goemon bowed his thanks. Both knew that he

might not return, but he was grateful for the older man's reticence and confidence in his decision.

I don't know who you are, thought Saizo as he turned away, but I am afraid you will never submerge yourself sufficiently to become a good merchant. For me too it was difficult. He thought of his dead friends and their deeds at Osaka and before, and his eyes welled with tears.

The road to the ancient capital of Miyako, which some people were now called simply Kyoto – Capital – was a pleasant walk from the bustling city of Osaka. Goemon walked through the fertile Yamato plain. The farmers were out, ploughing their fields with buffaloes. He passed the Taiko's former castle on Momovama Hill. He contrasted the peaceful scene before him with the time of the Osaka war, five years before. Then the farmers had not been able to plough in peace. Was their peace a worthy price to pay for the glory on the hill? Once he had been sure of the answer. That had been before he had become a doctor and known the people closely. Now he was not so sure.

The outskirts of Miyako came upon him gradually. He passed by the southern gate, so many times destroyed, so many times rebuilt. The streets became straight as arrows. The city had been built of old on a draughtboard pattern. It was surrounded by green-clad hills on three sides. Far to the northeast he could see Mount Hiei and the bulk of the monastery on its summit. Houses were hidden from view by dark wood fences. The people unlike the merchants of Osaka, were quiet, calm. There was little bustle. Behind the fences he could sense movement, life, but where he walked even the inevitable crowds seemed to suppress the excitement of living. He admired the temples and the pagoda towers that sprouted everywhere. It was a pleasure to be an unknown in a city he had known so well under other circumstance.

He completed his business with Saizo's correspondents quickly. At a loose end he wandered the markets and the roads of the city, not knowing what to expect. He was contemplating a display of hairpins, thinking longingly of Rosamund, when one of two lower-class samurai at a nearby booth chanced to look up.

The man looked casually at Goemon's merchant's garb, then focused on his face. There was a puzzled look on his for a moment, then excitement seized him. He grasped his companion's arm, and the other turned to look. Goemon, seeing his interest in him, turned his face and made his way quickly through the crowds. They forced their way after him rapidly. Seeing two hurrying samurai, people moved out of the way with alacrity. Goemon dodged through the crowds that impeded him more than his pursuers. He rounded a corner as they closed on him. A door before him opened. A figure stared at him a moment and beckoned. Without thinking, he dived through the open door and stood panting, peering through the slats. The two samurai turned the corner. Seeing he was out of sight, they conferred for a moment. They peered in every direction, rushed up the street and then back. When they could find no trace of their quarry they hurried off.

Goemon turned to face the girl Oko. Her small

197

face was as impassive as before, and she beckoned him to follow her.

The three travellers paused for a while at the head of the pass. Below them spread the straight intersecting streets of the city of Miyako. In the distance they could see the white-walled compound that was the home of the All Under Heaven. To their right rose the massive shoulder of Mount Hiei. A wild cherry tree was starting to bloom and spread its ancient branches over their head.

Okiku looked at the mountain beside them. Its summit was dotted with structures: the monastery of Mount Hiei. 'A bad place to fight,' she commented. Hachiro was on all their minds.

Jiro grinned. 'I have no intention of fighting there. I am not Two-Sword.'

She laughed and ruffled his topknot. Rosamund wanted to know what it was all about.

Several years before, Okiku told her, a man named Miyamoto Musashi had fought a duel against twenty men, and won. He was a famous swordsman now, his nickname deriving from the fact that he used a sword in either hand while fighting. Hachiro, they knew, had come to Miyako. They would have to separate him somehow, so that Jiro could face him in single combat. If he had his gang with him, Jiro had little chance, good though he had become under Ippei's peculiar modes of training.

They descended into the city and found lodging at a modest inn. They lay together, touching comfortably after a warm bath. Jiro relaxed completely, and dropped off. His would be the major burden in the following two days. Okiku looked at him for a long time. This might be the last eve of their life together, but she could not force her desires on him now. Rosamund lay and stared at nothing. Soon Jiro would kill whomever he had to. The reasons for it escaped her. Then they would be on their way to Osaka, and she would leave the shores of Japan, never to see Goemon again, never to feel his rough hands or hard cock. His face and figure rose before her eyes as her hand stole to her wet pussy. The man between them slept easily as the two women delicately rubbed their streaming pussies and ignored their streaming eyes. They climaxed together and fell into a deep sleep.

The room Goemon was ushered into overlooked a small garden. Small bushes overlooked a tiny pond stocked with expensive leopard-spotted carp. The widow from Kamakura was sitting by the window-sill. She bowed at his approach. Her face was slightly more lined than before. She was dressed in a fine silk robe; her hair was up in an elaborate hairdo. Tea utensils were set by her side.

Wordlessly she poured him a cup. He sipped. It was first-class brew, the first growth from around Sumpu, he judged.

'I am glad to see you again Goemon-san. Oko says she saw you being chased by two samurai. I see you are a merchant now.'

He moved uneasily, and laughed in embarrassment.

'I have changed my occupation, but not my person,' he said evasively.

199

'It appears other changes are in store for you if those samurai catch you.'

He nodded wordlessly.

'I have the feeling it is not what it seems,' she continued. 'They were not murderous in their intent. There is something strange here. I will consider it further at leisure.' She stretched out her hand and laid it on his crotch. His prick leaped erect.

'Indeed, you have not changed for the worse,' she said, smiling.

Oko swayed towards them, to perform her familiar office. She opened Goemon's robe and loin-cloth and exposed his rampant prick. Then she undid her mistress' wide embroidered sash and loosened her robes. The soft body emerged from its colourful inner cocoon. The widow leaned forward. She engulfed the head of Goemon's erection in her soft mouth, wetting it with her tongue. Then she shoved her head downwards, sucking in as much of his cock as she could. She raised her head and looked at his face.

'I want it forcefully now. There is much gentleness where I am going, but I want my body to taste your power.'

Vaguely troubled by her words, Goemon bowed in reply.

Oko brought several sitting pads and a pallet, which she spread on the floor. A charcoal brazier warmed the small room. The pads made a low flat mound at the head of the pallet. The widow laid herself on the mound so that her head and shoulders were raised. Oko directed Goemon, and he knelt on all fours, presenting his cock to the older woman's mouth. She fondled his pendent sack and erect manhood for a long while. He quivered at the gentle touch, but held his position. She stretched her neck forward and her lips encircled the crown of his pole, which she licked with the tip of her tongue.

'Fuck me now, hard!' she commanded.

He drew his knees in, then launched his hips forward. His cock slid down the length of her cavernous furnace of a mouth. She had drawn her teeth carefully behind her gums, and he barely felt their hardness scrape along his maleness. The crown slid along the bumps of her tongue which she arched to the meat against the arches of her palate. He pushed down deep into the throat, and she gagged. She controlled the reflex, urging him on with a tug on his balls.

His hairs tickled her nose, and she was full with the meat she had craved. He drew back, and rammed himself in again. She plied her tongue expertly against the most sensitive parts of his prick. He thrust in and out again and again, not caring about the sensitive tissues of her throat. Gratefully, she sucked at his penetration, though her throat began to burn at the pressure.

Oko bent before him. She raised the trailing skirts of her mistress' robes and exposed her full fleshy backside to Goemon's view. The deep dark crack ran away from his eyes, disappearing down the curve of the double hills. Even without the insistent pressure of Oko's hands, he knew what was expected of him. He lowered his head and gently licked the mounds before him. As his excitement mounted. His licks became more insistent and interspersed with bites. He moved himself harder and harder into her bruised mouth, and his teeth bit onto her ass mounds with insistent fury. He licked the length of the crack as far as he could reach, and then bit there too. She had bathed before his coming, and her musky smell rose cleanly and pleasantly in his nostrils. Oko's hand was roughly pummelling her mistress' cunt. She spread the pale legs wide, and then held the buttocks open. Goemon bit down, then searched with his long and mobile tongue. He rammed his tongue as far as it could reach into the exposed asshole. Her muscles fought him, but the insistent pecking of his tongue penetrated their defenses. His head swam with lust and he drove both his ends into the willing woman.

Suddenly she gave a strangled moan. Hearing it, he redoubled his frenzy. His balls started pumping in rhythm with her moans. His hairs mashed against her nose and he started spurting in long unending streams. She had little freedom of movement from the pressure. Almost fainting, her climax overtook her. Her body shook and trembled. She writhed under his assault. Her asshole relaxed as she came, and his tongue slipped in in victory. His spasms quieted down. Oko pulled him rapidly backwards. He fought her for a second until the last of his pearly cream had left his organ, then regaining his senses he pulled back.

The widow started breathing stertorously again. He examined her quickly. Her pulse was strong and her breathing returning. She came out of her faint rapidly. Oko handed her a restorative cup of tea, which she drank luxuriously. The widow looked at Goemon then.

'Strip!' she said.

Her eyes caressed his body at length, lingering with some disappointment on his flaccid shining tool. He divined her emotion, and by mere effort of will, he rose again. She smiled and motioned him closer. To make sure, she made a sign to Oko.

The maid had Goemon squat down. With soft hands she massaged his erect cock until it was rampant with lust. He knew better than to reach for her. Leaving him squatting, she attended to her mistress and stripped the robes off her. The widow lay on her side, bringing her upper leg up, knee close to her breast.

Again Oko led him by his prick to her side. He slid his prick the length of the widow's exposed leg. Oko separated her mistress' buttocks, raising one high, and the older woman herself pushed his cock into her relaxed cunt. The wetness from his tongue lubricated the experienced opening. She controlled his movements, pushing him in and drawing him out.

Finally, she pulled him out entirely. He trembled with effort and frustration at being deprived of his prey. Oko applied a sweet-smelling, dark orange cream to the loose opening.

'Persimmon extract,' smiled the widow over her shoulder. 'The astringency purses the muscles.'

She held his prick at her opening, and turned to look at the garden outside the window.

'Now,' she said. 'Fuck me again!'

He drove forward powerfully. The pursed muscles fought his intrusion. He remembered his penetration of Rosamund, and the feelings she had engendered in him rose again. The woman beneath him shrieked and he drove himself on. The head of his cock passed the pursed muscles and his shaft hurriedly followed. He rammed himself forward into her. The squishy feeling of her insides compensated his prick for the difficulty of entry. The hairs at the base of his manhood scraped painfully against her delicate ass. He drew himself back as far as he could and launched another rough attack. Again she cried out. He looked at her face. She was gazing wide-eyed at the garden, though whether she actually saw anything he did not know.

Oko slapped his rump.

'Harder. And faster!' she commanded.

He pumped himself roughly into the unresisting woman. Oko's hands roamed over his body, pleasuring him and urging him on when necessary. The woman clenched and unclenched her hands, and the muscles of her loins repeated the motion. Goemon was goaded beyond endurance. The sight of her body stretched out on her side encouraged his lust. He rammed fiercely into her. His hands scraped the length of her back and front. He clenched his hands over a soft breast, then dug a thumb roughly into her rounded hip. His other hand scraped against her back.

'Gently with your hands,' Oko admonished him.

'But not with your cock!' The widow gasped out. 'Not with your cock. Shove harder. Be a man!'

Goaded to further efforts, Goemon fought his way up her again and again. He was sweating now with effort. At last he felt his sperm beginning to rise. It took a long time, during which the pressure on his prick verged on pain. The woman under him was twitching now. Her outstretched leg was pushing against his imprisoning knees. She moaned again and again, and her eyes closed. The muscles on her belly shivered. Suddenly she stretched herself out full length. Her cunt constricted about Goemon's prick. She gave a hoarse cry, and he felt her juices flow. He discharged a minute after, a painfully slow spurt that nonetheless irrigated her insides copiously.

They lay together on the bed for a while. Oko served them some more tea, and then a strong broth brimming with fish and pounded-rice cakes. A sumo wrestler's stew. He saw it and laughed. The widow smiled at him warningly. 'The day is not over yet,' she said jokingly. 'There are still several matches to come.'

Oko brought tiny towels and led the two to the bath. It was an elaborate affair, overlooking the interior garden. Steaming water waited for them in a rock-studded pool. The maid washed her mistress first. She took care not to disturb Goemon's view. Using her hand, she soaped her mistress' cunt and fur. She turned her around and soaped the hole between the mounds of her mistress' buttocks. She laved the woman's tits gently, playing with the nipples. Using a rough cloth she then scrubbed her back. She sluiced hot water over the squatting woman, and the widow eased herself into the steaming water until only her head stuck out.

Oko washed Goemon as scrupulously. She redid his hair, and contrived to display him before her mistress. Goemon eased into the water after sluicing. He soaked gratefully for a while. The tension of being chased, the effort of the past hour, and the deeper tensions that he had carried with him were washed away with hot water.

He groped for the widow's water-slick body. She chuckled warmly.

'There is still more to come. Don't be impetuous. You will need this rest.'

He smiled at her. 'Why did you choose me a second time?' he asked.

'Isn't the fact that you have a nice body enough?'

He looked at her. She was not telling all the truth.

She understood his doubt. 'I am leaving this world,' she said unexpectedly. 'I am tired of fighting with my husband's relatives for his property. I am retiring to a nunnery, the Dosojin-ji in the Nanzan area. You might visit me someday.' She forbore to add anything else.

They dressed in light robes and returned to the room. Oko served them a lunch. The foods were all calculated to raise his energies, and remind him of his past efforts and future duties: fish roe, long giant radish stew, turtle meat.

When they finished, Oko played a flute and the other woman danced the stately dances of the imperial capital. They talked too. She had been born in the capital, and now, after her marriage was over, had returned to it before departing on another life. Her husband had been a lustful man, and had not hesitated, like many other husbands, to have his wife share his pleasures.

The dance ended. The widow seated herself beside Goemon.

'You must do something for me.'

He bowed in assent.

'I am leaving, but Oko must be cared for. There is something about you, something that makes me feel you will make her a good guardian. Her training is almost over. She has served me well, in bed and out. I wish you to have the use of her, and to keep her besides.'

'But I am only a poor itinerant doctor,' he protested.

'We both know that is not true,' she countered. 'Your carriage, your behaviour, the lines of your hands say otherwise. I will leave, but Oko will stay here until you are ready to take her.'

He bowed again. There was nothing he could say.

'She is a boiling pot,' warned the widow. 'I have stoked her fire carefully and continuously. I had thought that if I remarried again, as I grew older, she would keep my husband with me. Now that I have decided to retire, she will serve you. The last part of her early training is up to you, when you claim her. Observe.'

She had the young girl strip. Her breasts had grown since Goemon saw them last. His pulse quickened. She was a beautiful doll. Her mound had swelled. Pink lips between her legs were now more darkly fringed with hair, though the cunt was fully visible. She stared at them impassively, though Goemon now knew that the impassiveness hid fires of lustful anticipation. The widow took a long thin rod in one hand. She struck the girl's flank. A red welt rose, and Geomon's cock rose with it.

'She will not move. She is well trained, and she enjoys the sensations of her body. She will befit you.'

She turned to Goemon and with Oko's help

207

hastily stripped him. She rubbed herself over her entire body with his oozing prick. She sucked his stick and nibbled at the bag beneath. At last she laid herself on the pallet, legs spread.

He mounted her, and without preamble, plunged his hot rod into her waiting cavern. She was as tight as a virgin. Oko had spread some of the astringent ointment on the hole and lips. He forced her mightily, ignoring her protesting screams. She panted her lust into her face while crying out, 'No, no. Stop. I'm hurting.'

His hands kneaded her breasts and she tried to fight them off unsuccessfully. His strength and weight wore her down. She lay there passive under his onslaught, unable to move. Having emptied his balls before, Goemon felt no pressure to finish. He fucked her long and slowly, then at a more rapid pace, varying the depth and angle of his thrusts until her entire cunt had felt his presence. The pace of her breathing quickened. She stopped struggling. Her eyes rolled back in her head and a shy smile appeared on her lips. Her hips began jerking in response to his thrusts. Slowly, then more rapidly, she built up to a climax. Her face contorted. Long nails clawed at Goemon's back leaving red welts. Her moans were joyous now, not painful. The soft hole he was plugging was now slithery smooth, lubricated by her warm juices.

She jerked her hips several times and bit his lips as her climax overtook her. In no hurry, Goemon paused to watch the results of his work. Her face shone with sweat. Eyes half-closed and nostrils pinched, she shuddered at her internal sensations. At last her body relaxed. Without giving her pause, he began ploughing her juicy furrow again. She smiled up at him. 'That is what I expected.'

Oko leaned over them. She raised the woman's legs and crossed them over the man's sweating back. With a soft sash she bound them tightly in place. Goemon could not escape, and he continued his movement.

He lay on her the entire night. With hands and lips, and occasional slaps or blows from a brush, Oko and her mistress encouraged him to perform. He wondered at his unflagging manhood, and dully remembered the power of blowfish gonads, which he had undoubtedly drunk in his soup. The widow writhed under him, breathing endearments and happy cries. She came continuously, her legs supported by his body, crushing him to her. Oko fed him sugared fruit and cups of hot broth while he lay on the woman and performed.

The two women untied him in the grey light of morning. As the widow was donning the black-and-white robes of a nun, Goemon fell asleep. He did not notice her parting. He woke at noon, alone again. A new suit of clothes awaited him. The suit was not the dress of a commoner. Grey silk robe and striped silk over-trousers indicated the dress of a samurai of high rank. The family crest patches were missing. Under the clothes were two long, brocade-wrapped bundles. Opening them he was not surprised to see a pair of swords. Red lacquered sheaths winked at him. He withdrew the blades, with great expectations. The signature of one of the best smiths of four hundred years before – the classical period for swords – was embossed on the tang. Events seemed to be overtaking him. He dressed and reverently tucked the swords in his sash.

Oko was kneeling at the entrance. He approached without a word. Silently she proffered him a small object without a word. It was a small tobacco and medicine box held by a cord. Carved into the surface was a badge of intertwined willows. Noon sun and the crows of Miyako waited outside as he left.

CHAPTER 16

A spring sun gently warmed the streets of Miyako.
Jiro and the two girls had been searching for traces
of Hachiro since the early morning. Okiku, who
knew all the stews and hiding holes of the city, was
the one who had found the traces. Hachiro, they
knew, was bound to pass by the bridge on his way
to the Arakawa river, on the banks of which some
of his gang awaited him. He himself was too clever
to ever appear on the police lists, but many of
his men were wanted. Noon came. Okiku tensed
expectantly. Down one of the alleys that debouched
into the clearing before the red-painted bridge they
were standing on she could hear the strains of a
male voice singing a well-known melody. This time
there was no ambivalence. Her man stood beside
her, and the other was just a man she wanted to
kill. She remembered the night Hachiro and his
men had burst into her family's house. Her father
had been in the service of Hattori Hanzo, spy-
master to Tokugawa Ieyasu. He had trusted
Hachiro, even betrothed his daughter to him.
Hachiro was interested in gold, and loyalties were
not his concern. He knew Okiku's father was being
paid well, and he took the opportunity to secure

211

the gold by treachery. Hachiro's men, outnumbering her family, had won. She had escaped to secure the assistance of her uncle, Ippei. They returned to find only the dead. Now was the time for revenge. She smiled grimly.

Hachiro strode proudly forward from between two houses. He reached the centre of the area before the bridge, and Jiro slid forward.

'You are Hachiro, I believe?' enquired the giant courteously.

Hachiro stopped motionless. His wide eyes took in the scene before him in one glance. A lone samurai, a nun, and a familiar figure stood before him. He smiled at Okiku.

'Chrysanthemum dolls should be seen in the autumn, not in spring,' he said, laughing.

'This chrysanthemum is about to kill you,' she answered, hate smouldering in her eyes. Her hands twisted, and her straight blade was suddenly in her hand. The staff sheath clattered to the ground.

'I was always better than you,' said Hachiro mockingly. 'You are only a woman after all. You could have been mine, with all the privileges. Now I'll have you anyway and leave you to my men.'

Her eyes blazed at the taunt. She screamed and started to charge.

'Okiku!' rumbled the giant beside her, and she subsided. Hachiro's gaze shifted to Jiro. 'Well, big man, you were a sorry sight last time I saw you, bawling like a child and flailing your arms.'

Jiro didn't answer. He slid forward again, and his great two-handed curved sword slithered out of its scabbard. He held it at his side with one hand. Okiku and Rosamund followed him off the bridge, keeping behind him. Hachiro glanced behind them to keep them off balance.

'You expect to fight me? In single combat? Don't be silly, samurai, ninja do not do such things.' He smiled at them broadly as a group of ruffians rushed off the bridge and surrounded the three vengeance-seekers. Hachiro laughed loud and drew his sword. He had powerful hands with hairy knuckles, and as he reversed the sword, blade pointing back along his arm, hilt extended, light flashed on the loose armour shirt he wore beneath his heavy brown jacket. Jiro did nothing but take a breath and adjust his stance. Around them, townspeople rushed for cover, some peering fearfully out from shuttered doors or behind corners. They wished to see the spectacle, but when the city governor's runners arrived on the scene, there would be indiscriminate arrests. Since the governor had just died, it would be a long while before release, even for mere bystanders.

It was Rosamund who was the first to take action. She and Okiku were standing more or less back to back, protecting Jiro's rear. Facing her were four men. One, a dirty, heavily bearded man with a broken nose, was reaching for her. The other three were leisurely drawing swords. They looked tough and competent, not like most of the rest of the gang, and they carried themselves with the erect stride of ex-soldiers. Rosamund screamed and lashed down with her hand. The weighted chain she had concealed in her fist – a gift from Ippei who had also taught her its use – lashed out. The octagonal weight struck the robber on the temple. He fell without a sound. She whirled and lashed the kusari out again at the closest of the four men. He avoided her and stepped back, and she recovered. She loosened her robes to give her some freedom, and a sword blade sliced at her waist. It cut through her sash, and her gown opened. Something fell to the ground with a clatter. She ignored it as she moved backwards, out of range. One of the men stared at the fallen object in surprise. His eyes were caught by the device of six coins embossed on it. He called out to the man who had cut at Rosamund.

'That comes from Lord Sanada! Where did she get it?'

One of them recovered the small box. He opened it deftly. Inside was a slip of paper, scrawled with one sentence in black ink. It was stamped with a red seal in the shape of a gourd.

'Assist this woman,' read out the man who was holding the paper. He looked at Rosamund with something like respect, and raised the message to his forehead. The three men, former retainers of the commander of the Tokugawa opponents in the Osaka War, bowed to the message. They ranged themselves round Rosamund, defending her against their robber associates.

Rosamund's screaming attack precipitated the fight in earnest. Okiku's left hand darted into the folds of her robe. A swarm of glittering stars flew through the air. Two of the robbers screamed. One had a star-shaped knife embedded in his eye, another's wrist was spurting blood. With a leap, she attacked the nearest robber. Her straight blade cut forward in a feint, withdrew, then stabbed at his unprotected belly. It went in deep. She withdrew with a tug and a twist, turned on one heel, and rammed the hilt of her sword into the kidney of a man about to stab Jiro from behind.

As the fight started, Hachiro, still with a mocking smile on his face, leaped backwards. Two of his men rushed forward in his stead. Jiro's sword swept up without any warning. A robber's hand flopped in the dust. The sword swept down and a gush of blood flew from the second attacker's severed artery.

'Well big man, you've improved a bit,' said Hachiro, stepping over his dying men. His sword flashed as he leaped. Jiro ducked slightly, and a wisp of hair flew from his top-knot.

Hachiro chuckled. 'Good barbering eh? I'll shave you much closer.'

The Sanada men had finished their hurried council. Without a word, they attacked their former comrades. Several robbers fell. The Sanada men ranged themselves by Rosamund, protecting her with their bodies. The fight raged on. One of the Sanada men fell, stabbed by a fallen robber.

The odds were better now, but the robbers were getting the better of the bargain. Jiro received a scratch from a robber he had killed almost contemptuously as he stalked Hachiro. Okiku received a cut on her foot. Rosamund was the only one who was protected for some time, but the Sanada men were wounded again and again, and one of them fell. Only their leader remained. Panting, the combatants paused for a moment.

Jiro looked around. The two girls were still standing. Robber corpses littered the ground, but there were more standing. He wiped all thoughts –

of Okiku, of Rosamund, of himself – from his mind. His shoulders squared. He gripped his sword calmly and his eyes met Hachiro's. The robber chieftain grinned mockingly. His was the victory. He stepped out ahead of his men who were ringing his prey.

'Now, you die.' His sword glinted evilly as he raised it.

Goemon wandered through the streets of Miyako. People made way for him as he strode with resumed dignity through the streets. He paused outside the west gate of the governor's mansion, looking at it thoughtfully, then walked off to the west. The sight of the river had induced calm in him since childhood.

He rounded a corner near the river, and a group of grim samurai, hurrying in the same direction, noted his passing. One of them yelled something, and they pelted in his direction, 'Wagadono!' 'Wagadono!' they yelled in frustration as he slipped through the crowd.

Before him the road led to a bridge over one of the canals. There appeared to be a brawl going on in the area before the bridge. He strode on, concerned with his own affairs, when the sight he saw crystallised in his mind. Jiro, sword blood-stained, was facing an armed man in brown. A girl with her back to him must be Okiku. She was screaming and cutting efficiently with a straight sword. Beside them stood a sight he had longed for for many months. Rosamund, a tight look on her face, a strange man by her side, was facing part of the circle of rough-looking attackers. There was no mistaking her. Her nun's coif had fallen off and her blonde hair blew about. As he ran towards her, the man defending her fell from a sword thrust. She turned to run, and he saw that her sash had been cut. Her beautiful body came in view. Her full breasts jounced, and her white thighs flashed as on the day he first met her. Old skills came back to Goemon. His sword was out of its scabbard and through the neck of one attacker before he had even thought of the action. He raced forward, past Rosamund, and his sword sliced again and again through meat and bone. Rosamund's attackers fell, and Goemon turned to strike at others just as a mass of official uniforms boiled into the square.

Hachiro and Jiro were only marginally aware of Goemon's attack. They faced each other, intent on the next few seconds. As Goemon's pursuers burst into the square, Hachiro attacked. He leaped into the air, his feet at the height of Jiro's head. As he jumped, sharp darts flew from his left hand. Easily, as if he were merely swaying on a whim, Jiro avoided the darts. He slid forward, drawn by his sword, and cut once. Hachiro reached the ground and slumped. His side opened and a flood of dark blood stained the ground. He groaned one, tried to grin, and died. Behind him, Jiro froze, his sword at the end of his outstretched arm.

He was knocked suddenly to the ground. Rough hands bound him and wrenched the sword from his grasp. Grim-faced samurai, some carrying red corded batons – the mark of police – surrounded him. He looked around him. Rosamund was hemmed in by a ring of policemen. Her white body flashed from her open robe. Okiku was being tied up efficiently by several policemen, but her eyes were only for Jiro. A small circle of samurai were surrounding Goemon. Their swords were out, though they were facing away from him. Before him, fists clenched as if held in the grip of great emotion, stood an elderly samurai.

Rosamund glanced down at a sound. At her feet, the leader of the Sanada men who had come to her rescue was trying to speak. She knelt at his head. 'Tell him . . .' gasped the man, 'Tell . . . him . . . . Tell Lord Sanada that we fulfilled his command to the death.' His head fell back and he died. Gently she closed his eyes before she too was bound. Ahead of her, she finally saw Goemon. He was being rushed off encircled by guards, and she wondered what lay in store for all of them.

The courtroom was a wide hall with a broad platform filling one third of it. At the back of the platform was a wide double sliding door. Guards armed with staves stood behind the prisoners. Two samurai knelt before the double doors.

Jiro knelt and considered his actions. He had acted correctly, he knew. Revenge was a sacred duty, he was a samurai, and he had nothing to fear. He stole a look in Rosamund's direction. That was the problem. Though the punishment against foreigners travelling unlicensed through the empire was, for the present at least, loosely enforced, there might have been a change in policy. And she was most definitely a kirisitan. And the mystery of Goemon intrigued him. What had the doctor done to be arrested with them in such a fashion?

The clerk, who was kneeling on the platform, an

elderly samurai, called out 'Matsudaira Konosuke, Intendant of the Shogun in Miyaki, will judge the prisoners.' The guards growled at the prisoners and the three of them hastily touched their foreheads to the floor.

The double doors opened. The Governor of Miyako entered. His long formal trousers trailed behind him on the floor, forcing him to walk in a shuffle that flipped them behind him like the tail of a fish. He wore a wide-shouldered overcoat of silk, and a colourful silk robe tucked into his trousers. The handle of his short sword was wound with white braid. His topknot divided his shaven pate like a sword blade.

'You may sit up,' said the governor in a deep official voice.

Jiro's eyes travelled up the length of the figure before him. He noted the rich fittings, the official signs of power. His eyes reached those of the governor's and he froze in shock.

Rosamund looked at the governor and gasped. It was Goemon. She started to rise, and the governor quelled her with a fierce look. She looked at him in adoration. He had never been so fierce, so glorious, as he appeared to her now.

'Miura Jiro, brawling in public streets is forbidden. However, since you are a samurai, and since I understand it was an affair of revenge, and since you have reported this revengeful act, and since the man you killed was a wanted robber, Hachiro by name, I merely sentence you to banishment from your home of Muira.'

Jiro looked at his erstwhile friend in bewilderment.

'The woman Okiku,' continued Goemon implacably. 'It is unseemly for a woman to be without a guardian. You are hereby placed in the custody of a samurai, one Miura Jiro, who will be responsible for your conduct.' Okiku bowed deeply in reply.

Goemon turned to face Rosamund. His topknot flashed darkly in the light.

'The woman Rosamund. You are a foreigner who has been wandering through our provinces without official permission. You are to be incarcerated for that crime. The House of Matsudaira will be responsible for that incarceration, and for administering suitable physical chastisement whenever necessary.'

The illustrious figure of the governor rose to its full height. He turned with a flourish and kicked the long trailing lengths of his trousers behind him. The double doors opened before him and he stalked through. Rosamund, the only one who had not bowed deeply enough, was the only one to see the governor's quick wink as he turned.

She waited in the sumptuously-appointed room. It was decorated with screens painted with lifesize cherry trees in full bloom. The back wall held a painting of a hawk on a pine tree. There were soft padded seating cushions, and a small lacquered bureau held a vase with an arrangement of spring flowers.

She was still dressed in her nun's robes, without a sash. Her hands were tied behind her back by a rope that wound around her body and bit into her tits. They were painful now, irritated by the silken ropes, and her nipples stiffened against the pressure. Her blonde hair, free now, fell to her shoulders.

A door slid open. The many lit candles shone on the figure of Goemon. He was dressed in a plain white cotton robe held by a plain blue sash. He held a sword sheathed in red lacquer at his side. He looked at her dishevelled state for a while, and the tension grew. She looked back at him, without a word. Inside her the juices gathered. She knew what was to come, waited for it expectantly. He licked his lips. Slowly he knelt and placed the sword on the floor. He untied his sash and dropped sash and robe. His huge maleness stood up from the nest of black hairs, questing for her like a snake. She tucked her legs under her, and the sight of her white knees flashing into view brought on explosive action.

With one lunge he threw her on her back on the floor. She kicked out at him and he grunted in pain as she landed on his thigh. He slapped her beautiful thighs once, then again. Pink stains marred her white skin. He clenched her ankles between his knees, and forcefully tore her knees apart. He slapped at her revealed pink and gold mound, and his hand landed with a wet splat. Her cunt was open to him. Long pink lips headed by the erect clitoris. All was framed by silky, long golden curls. Another flash of colour caught his eyes. He bent forward to see, and she spread her legs wider to allow him the view he craved. On her right thigh was tattooed the beautiful image of a red rose in full bloom. The stem flowered out of her cunt hole, and the petals partly obscured the lip. A tiny fresh leaf ran back to touch the puckered hole of her anus. He wondered who the artist was, the rose was so lifelike.

Suddenly she clamped her legs together. Caught between these alabaster pillars, the governor of the city of Miyako did the only thing he could. He lunged forward. His tongue stabbed into the beautiful pussy before him. He bit and licked at the perfect lips as Rosamund twisted and moaned, never letting go her hold. His hands clawed at her ass. He dug stiff fingers into the soft mounds, then into the hole between. He struck her again and again on the buttocks, and she responded with grunts and happy squeals.

At last he pried her knees from around his face. His ears hurt and flamed a bright red. She looked at his face and laughed. He grinned savagely, and rolled her so that her beautiful white ass stuck into the air. With a flat hand he began slapping her buttocks. His hand left pink imprints on the white rounded surfaces. Gradually, like buns browning in an overn, her ass turned a bright pink. The smell of her cunt rose in his nostrils as her juices sluiced down her cunt. Hastily he rolled over. She opened her knees willingly and he plunged between them.

His tumescent member thrust between her fat lips. He was unstoppable. With one lunge he had penetrated her to her depths. His hands clawed at her flaming buttocks, and he ground himself into her. She started coming and he saw her eyes rolling in her head.

'I love you Goemon, I love you,' she repeated again and again as she climaxed. The pleasure had no end. Her thighs gripped his hips, and her cunt, still in the throes of its own pleasure, began milking

222

him with a pressure he knew he could not resist. Frantically he reached out a hand and seized the short sword he had dropped earlier. He raised it high and brought it down onto her trembling body.

The ropes that bound her fell apart at the exact cut of the sword. Her tits popped out, released from their bondage. They aimed pink nipples at his face. He grinned at her savagely and threw the sword aside. As his own climax approached, he slapped her newly-released breasts thoroughly until they were as pink as her backside. She howled with joy. She pulled him to her. Her hungry mouth fastened on his and he drove his tongue savagely into her mouth. She came again together with him, and he collapsed on her soft body, her muscular cunt holding him to her in a soft-jawed vice.

They lay there, gently breathing and murmuring to one another. Their juices ran between her legs. She scratched and stroked his sweaty body lovingly.

'Who are you?,' she said wonderingly. Then she hugged him in sudden energy, and her cunt squeezed his cock roughly until his maleness began rising again. 'I don't care. I'm with you and I'll not let you go.'

He laughed. 'Well, you definitely have me.' His voice became serious. 'My father was governor of Miyako. We are a junior branch of the Shogun's family. I quarrelled with him during and after the Osaka war. I thought the Tokugawa opponent's claims were just. My father disagreed. Two years ago I escaped Miyako, and have been wandering since, trying to get my thoughts together. Now I know that my father was right. It is too late to revive the old quarrel, whichever side is right. It is

223

better to have peace for the people. I came back to tell him so. He died some weeks ago. I have inherited his position.'

She looked at him sombrely. 'What of me?'

He grinned, 'I am justice here. I will have an impressive House of Women. I can keep whom I want there. And I want you.'

With his last words he drove into her with renewed energy. She countered him happily. They wrestled on the floor. His cock slipped out of her in the struggle. Biting and slapping, he forced her back. She opened her legs and exposed her colourful cunt to his gaze again. He kneeled before her deliberately. He took careful aim with one hand on his pulsing lance. The tip touched the waiting hole, and she clenched her internal muscles. He shoved, and the tip did not move in. Enraged, he pulled at her hips. The tip barely penetrated. She smiled at him.

'Only when I let you, lover.'

He leaned down and bit her nipple. Deliberately he bit the other one. She still smiled and gazed at him without a quiver. He rammed at her with all his might, and still her barriers held. He held off, panting. His demanding thrusts changed to a pleading. His cock slipped up and down her hairy twat, begging for entrance.

'Please Rosamund, please.' Involuntarily his breathing had turned to a prayer. She clawed his chest. 'Now you may,' she breathed in a whisper.

The slide down her cunt was like nothing he had ever experienced before. She relaxed her muscles slowly, beginning at the entrance to her slick hole. He had to struggle every bit of the way, but the muscular walls of her cunt held him tightly as the tip forced its way in. It was, he decided, like having a virgin a hundred times over.

As their hairs joined he could no longer hold back. She gave one single quick squeeze the length of his organ, and the remains of his sperm squirted out, drenching her interior. He wriggled on her torso like a hooked fish, and in satisfaction. Knowing her victory, she joined him.

They lay together. Goemon slowly recovering, when Rosamund sensed another presence in the room. She turned her head. A slim young girl was kneeling at the entrance to the room. Goemon too turned his head.

'That is Oko,' he said. The young girl was entirely naked. Long black hair flowed down her back. Her small breasts rose and fell gently with her breathing.

'She was given to me. She is a virgin. She is yours if you want her,' breathed Goemon in her ear.

Rosamund rolled him off her and raised herself on her elbow.

'Come here,' she said.

Oko rose and floated towards them. She knelt at Rosamund's head. Without willing it, her hand snaked forth to stroke the golden halo that lay on the floor.

'Did you see everything we did?' asked the blonde.

The young girl nodded.

'Did you like it?' Oko nodded again. 'Even the blows? the biting? the screams?'

'Yes, oh yes.'

Without removing her eyes from the girl, Rosamund said, 'Show me how much you liked it, Oko.'

The slim girl parted her legs. She stroked her pussy gently, and drops of pearly dew formed on the delicate lips. Her other hand stole to her tits, and pinched each tiny black nipple hard between her fingers. Her face remained impassive though her body trembled. Rosamund leaned over and lowered her head to the juncture of the girl's thighs. Suddenly she bit the smooth skin until she could taste blood. There was a quiver and a moan from the girl, but she did not move away, nor did she cease frigging herself. Rosamund bit the girl again, on the other thigh, then drew back. There were two bright red marks on the flawless skin of each inner thigh, bright buds that complemented the tattooed blooming rose on Rosamund's thighs.

'She will be mine. I love her already.' A sob escaped Oko and her eyes cried her gratitude.

Goemon watched in fascination. Rosamund bent and licked the delicate young hand, then pushed it aside and licked the juices off the almost hairless lower lips. Oko froze and tensed. Her legs spread wider, and her face was now controlled again. Rosamund pulled back. She looked at Oko in admiration. Hastily she slipped behind the girl. She pulled her back until Oko rested on her full cushiony tits. Large full nipples dug gently into the slim girl's back. Rosamund pinched the tight little nipples until they stood out more prominently. She kissed and mouthed the girls ears.

'Now, Goemon!' she commanded suddenly.

He lunged forward. His erect manhood broke through the girl's virgin barrier. Without pause he rammed up her tight channel. He was in a delirium now. The girl lay under him passively, leaning back on Rosamund and awaiting her orders. Her eyes were alight with lust. Moans escaped her lips involuntarily.

'Yes, yes. Don't stop. I've been waiting for so long for you,' she gasped. He pulled her to him by her buttocks, his hands bruising the buttery surfaces. He bit at her nipples and belly, and then his mouth met Rosamund's and he thrust his tongue almost down her throat.

'Where is Jiro?' the blonde whispered at him fiercely. She repeated the question until it finally penetrated.

'In a room two doors down,' he finally gasped.

'Get up!' she commanded him urgently.

'What?' he asked in a daze.

'Get up! No! Don't withdraw from her.'

Goemon picked Oko up, still connected at their hips. The girl curled her legs around him. Led by Rosamund they made their way through the doors.

Jiro and Okiku were huddled together on a pallet. There was no question what they had been doing. They scrambled to their knees. Rosamund hurled herself on Jiro and rolled him over. Before he could recover she sat on his chest and announced in loud tones:

'I have a message from Matsudaira Konosuke. He cannot be present, but commands that his physician, Goemon, be here with us whenever necessary.'

Goemon was the first to grasp her point. He bowed awkwardly to Jiro.

'Jiro-san, I am happy to see you again after so

227

many months. I will try not to lose track of you again. In fact, if you reside in Miyako, I will make the effort to see you as often as Lord Matsudaira allows.'

Understanding dawned on the other two. They smiled conspiratorially. The lives of senior officials were bound about by ceremony and duty, and everyone had a need to relax away from them. This was an unusual device, but it would keep the four of them together.

Jiro pointed at Oko, still hanging from Goemon's waist. 'I see your prick has grown somewhat since the last time.'

'He actually wants some help with that,' Rosamund broke in. She raised Jiro to his feet. She and Okiku started sucking at the young giant's slick cock, slightly softened now by use. It soon rose in glory. Oko watched, her face impassive but apprehension mirrored in the tension of her body. Okiku slowly apprached Oko. She bent and spread the thin buttocks. A touch of her tongue sent thrills of fear and expectation through her frame. Goemon's cock was still resting, quiet but expectant in her cunt.

The two girls led Jiro forward. No instructions were necessary. While the girls spread Oko's ass, pulling each small bun to a different side, he gently presented his engorged cock.

The serving girl quivered as, with infinite care, the two men sank to their knees, then lay on the floor on their sides, the girl prisoned between them. Rosamund twisted the girl until her lust-glazed eyes were looking into her own blue ones. She kissed the feverish brow softly, and was rewarded by a blinding, loving smile. She reversed herself and thrust her projecting clit into the girl's hungrily sucking mouth. A male mouth closed on her ass, biting and licking deep. Another bit and nibbled her perfectly-shaped stomach.

Okiku watched the scene for a moment, debating which end to join. It was going to be an interesting life for the four of them, she decided, as she made her choice.

Miura Anjin died that same spring. Miura Jiro and his wife settled in Miyako where he became a teacher. They were frequently visited by Goemon and by Rosamund, dressed as a nun. They would disappear for short periods from their home, and the number of residents of the House of Women of Matsudaira Konosuke, Governor of Miyako for may years, grew apace. Ippei, in the manner of yamabushi, ate pine needles and bark for ninety days and was translated into a buddha in this life. Miyamoto Musashi, swordsman, painter, sculptor, died of old age and became the 'Sword Saint' of Japan. Tokugawa Ieyasu died content, his country at peace. His dynasty survived for seventeen generations, and presided over two hundred years of almost complete peace.

NEXUS ADULT READS

ANONYMOUS AUTHORS

0352314850	**The Adventures of a Schoolboy**	**£2.50**
0352313269	**Beatrice**	**£2.99***
0352314915	**The Boudoir**	**£2.99***
0352317884	**Confessions of an English Maid**	**£2.75***
0352322152	**The Devils Advocate**	**£2.95**
0352317221	**Eroticon**	**£2.99**
0352318627	**Eroticon II**	**£2.99**
0352321660	**Eroticon III**	**£2.99**
0352313374	**Eveline**	**£2.99***

Nexus books are obtainable from many booksellers and newsagents. If you have any difficulty tick the titles you want and fill in the form below.

Name _____

Address _____

Send to: Nexus Cash Sales, P.O. Box 11, Falmouth, Cornwall TR10 9EN.

Please send a cheque or postal order to the value of the cover price plus:
UK: 55p for the first book, 22p for the second book and 14p for each additional book ordered to the maximum charge of £1.75.

BFPO and EIRE: 55p for the first book, 22p for the second book, 14p per copy for the next 7 books, thereafter 8p per book.

OVERSEAS: £1.00 for the first book and 25p per copy for each additional book.

While every effort is made to keep prices low, it is sometimes necessary to increase prices at short notice. Nexus reserve the right to show new retail prices on covers which may differ from those advertised in the text or elsewhere.

* NOT FOR SALE IN CANADA

NEXUS ADULT READS

0352322454	**Forbidden Frolics**	**£2.99**
0352322004	**The French Collection**	**£2.95**
0352317817	**Exploits of a Young Don Juan**	**£2.50**
0352318554	**Flossie**	**£2.99***
0352313390	**'Frank' and I**	**£2.99***
0352316667	**Lascivious Scenes**	**£2.99***
035231530X	**Laura Middleton**	**£2.99***
0352315830	**The Lustful Turk**	**£2.99***
0352310170	**A Man With A Maid**	**£2.99***
0352310928	**A Man With A Maid Vol II**	**£2.99***

Nexus books are obtainable from many booksellers and newsagents. If you have any difficulty tick the titles you want and fill in the form below.

Name _____

Address _____

_____

Send to: Nexus Cash Sales, P.O. Box 11, Falmouth, Cornwall TR10 9EN.

Please send a cheque or postal order to the value of the cover price plus:
UK: 55p for the first book, 22p for the second book and 14p for each additional book ordered to the maximum charge of £1.75.

BFPO and EIRE: 55p for the first book, 22p for the second book, 14p per copy for the next 7 books, thereafter 8p per book.

OVERSEAS: £1.00 for the first book and 25p per copy for each additional book.

While every effort is made to keep prices low, it is sometimes necessary to increase prices at short notice. Nexus reserve the right to show new retail prices on covers which may differ from those advertised in the text or elsewhere.

* *NOT FOR SALE IN CANADA*

NEXUS ADULT READS

0352313781	**A Man With a Maid Vol III**	**£2.99***
0352316209	**Maudie**	**£2.25**
0352314826	**The Memoirs of Dolly Morton**	**£2.25**
0352313692	**More Eveline**	**£2.99***
0352318457	**A Night in a Moorish Harem**	**£2.50***
0352311355	**Oh Wicked Country!**	**£2.25**
0352316756	**Parisian Frolics**	**£2.25***
0352320494	**Pleasure Bound**	**£2.95**
0352315687	**Randiana**	**£2.99***

Nexus books are obtainable from many booksellers and newsagents. If you have any difficulty tick the titles you want and fill in the form below.

Name _____

Address _____

_____

Send to: Nexus Cash Sales, P.O. Box 11, Falmouth, Cornwall TR10 9EN.

Please send a cheque or postal order to the value of the cover price plus:
UK: 55p for the first book, 22p for the second book and 14p for each additional book ordered to the maximum charge of £1.75.

BFPO and EIRE: 55p for the first book, 22p for the second book, 14p per copy for the next 7 books, thereafter 8p per book.

OVERSEAS: £1.00 for the first book and 25p per copy for each additional book.

While every effort is made to keep prices low, it is sometimes necessary to increase prices at short notice. Nexus reserve the right to show new retail prices on covers which may differ from those advertised in the text or elsewhere.

* NOT FOR SALE IN CANADA

NEXUS ADULT READS

0352312327	**The Romance of Lust Book I**	£2.99*
035231267X	**The Romance of Lust Book II**	£2.99*
035231544X	**Rosa Fielding**	£2.25*
0352311312	**Suburban Souls Book I**	£2.25*
0352311762	**Suburban Souls Book II**	£2.50*
0352314605	**Three Times A Woman**	£2.99*
0352317809	**Violette**	£2.50
0352317299	**The Fiesta Letters**	£2.50
0352316438	**The Fiesta Book of Saucy Crosswords**	£1.95
035231852X	JANE ANNE ROBERTS **The Secret Web**	£2.50

Nexus books are obtainable from many booksellers and newsagents. If you have any difficulty tick the titles you want and fill in the form below.

Name _____

Address _____

_____

Send to: Nexus Cash Sales, P.O. Box 11, Falmouth, Cornwall TR10 9EN.

Please send a cheque or postal order to the value of the cover price plus: UK: 55p for the first book, 22p for the second book and 14p for each additional book ordered to the maximum charge of £1.75.

BFPO and EIRE: 55p for the first book, 22p for the second book, 14p per copy for the next 7 books, thereafter 8p per book.

OVERSEAS: £1.00 for the first book and 25p per copy for each additional book.

While every effort is made to keep prices low, it is sometimes necessary to increase prices at short notice. Nexus reserve the right to show new retail prices on covers which may differ from those advertised in the text or elsewhere.

* NOT FOR SALE IN CANADA